A Promise Kept
and Other Stories

by
Dennis Deitz

Printed in the United State of America
The Printing Press, Ltd., Charleston, WV

A Promise Kept and Other Stories
formerly
The Lost Years and Other Stories
Copyright 1994, J. Dennis Deitz
ISBN 0-938985-12-4

Published by
Mountain Memories Books
216 Sutherland Drive
South Charleston, West Virginia 25303

Table of Contents

Dedication ii

Introduction iii

Foreword v

A Promise Kept 1
Could you have kept, or accepted, this promise?

Joe's Song 10
By Vera Taylor

Rainbow of Seasons 12
By Vera Taylor

Catherine's Song 14
By Vera Taylor

A Promise Kept: Play Adaptation 17

The Rescue: Part One "Tom's Story" 48
Tom's love of hearing stories comes in handy when the
girl he loves is captured by Indians.

The Rescue: Part Two "Molly's Story" 65
Can a sixteen-year-old girl outwit a whole band of Indians?

John Lane's Story 85
Two little boys with big dreams head north to find
work and find much more than they had hoped for.

The Teacher 121
You can do more than you ever dreamed of when
someone special believes in you.

Years of Solid Gold 143
Sharon is only nine years old when she decides she
will marry Jimmy.

Years of Solid Gold 149
A poem by Vera Taylor

Going out for the Mail 154
A piece of mail can change your life.

The Lost Years 156
What do you do when your wife and children are
beautiful, but you can't remember anything about them?

Dedication

Dedicated to my wife Madeline
and our children
Joyce, Jaye, and Linda Kay.

Introduction

I had heard stories of Dennis Deitz long before I was privileged to met him. My mother, Garnette James Bragg, grew up near the Deitz family in the Hickory Flats area near Russellville in Greenbrier County. Understandably, my impressions of Dennis were colored by my mother's recollections of their youthful escapades. In the early 1970's when I finally met Dennis and his wife Madeline, I was surprised by the man who was introduced. Expecting to meet the original Dennis the Menace, I was delighted to encounter a gracious, witty, and hospitable gentleman. That introduction proved to be a highlight of my life, for I learned that although Dennis had grown into a courteous, compassionate man, glimpses of the impish boy were still very evident.

Dennis and my mother grew up in a much simpler time, in an area that today is described as extremely rural. What we might view as hardships were accepted in those days as the experiences of everyday life. No indoor plumbing, no electricity, no convenient stores to purchase bread and milk--the lack of these modern-day necessities wasn't considered a hardship. Each person, adult and child alike, had a role to play in the day-to-day life of the family, and that role was carried out without complaint. Television hadn't come on the scene and entertainment was a self-taught event. Taking an ordinary event and embellishing it into an elaborate tale was a great art and provided hours of enjoyment for long winter evenings.

Dennis and his buddy Frank James were masters at the art of storytelling. Dennis sometimes had a hand in creating the event (chasing his sisters and their friends with a blacksnake), which Frank then wove into an elaborate tale. Even an ordinary walk through the woods might be transformed into a story of Dennis and Frank fighting their way through a forest filled with ghosts, goblins, and other hair-raising creatures.

Let me tell you a little about Dennis, the boy, and you'll see why I was unprepared for the man I eventually met.

Dennis' sister Helen was my mother's closest friend, and Mother spend much of her time at the Deitz home. The rambling two-story farmhouse, I understand, often shook with the shouts and pounding footsteps of children at all hours of the day and night.

After one particularly long day spent with the Deitz family, Mother began her nearly two-mile walk home. The summer sun had been swallowed by the mountains, and twilight was quickly fading into night. Kids growing up in the country during that pre-Depression era didn't think of muggers, murderers, or other villains we seem to encounter on a daily basis in our present-day world; in those times, a walk through the cool night was actually a treat. As she strolled the dirt road that wound through the hills, Mother listened to the crickets as they began their serenade, and she watched the rustling leaves as they tried to catch the first moonbeams filtering through the trees. An occasional bird peeped out a good night to its friends as the woods settled into a comforting, tranquil wait for the dawn.

Absorbed in her thoughts, Mother was in no hurry to conclude her journey home. As she rounded a slight turn, her revery was shattered as a ghostly apparition arose from the weeds lining the road. The figure moaned and groaned as it began moving toward her.

I'm a city-raised kid, through and through. Had it been me in my mother's shoes, I would have fainted or at least made a mad sprint in the opposite direction. Not Mother. She scooped a handful of rocks from the road and began pelting the "haint." The missiles had an immediate effect, for the unearthly figure quickly turned human and a voice yelled, "Stop, Garnie, stop! It's me--Dennis!" Only after she was sure it wasn't the Devil himself did Mother stop her bombardment. I can only guess at the aftermath, but I'm sure Dennis thought twice before he played another prank on my mother!

A bit of the mischievous boy still peeks through in many of Dennis's writings today as he chronicles his life of growing up country--growing up in a simpler time and place and with family and friends who have remained true throughout the years. His stories and compilations have delighted countless readers, including this one, and his latest effort is no exception--I'm sure you'll be entertained. Dennis is truly an inspiring writer, one who recognizes the importance of our heritage and the value of family. I'm honored to call him a friend, but I'm sure glad he grew up before my time--I'm a real coward!

--Sara Bragg Stricker

Foreword

With the stories in this collection, Dennis Deitz has accomplised several things:

He has written colorful and interesting accounts of *the lives of good people*--a rarity in much of today's fiction.

He has captured past times in a storyteller's voice, personalizing history for the younger generation.

He has depicted loving, respectful relationships between men and women, and has shown the happiness that can come to husbands and wives who value one another for their minds, bodies, and good hearts.

He has written a broad range of stories--a twist on a modern detective story ("The Lost Years"), a humorous essay ("Going Out for the Mail"), and stories that touch key events in Appalachian folklore and history--being captured by Indians and living during civil war times.

He has written stories that can teach us to be better people. In "The Teacher," we see that many good things come about because one man--The Teacher--takes a special interest in a little boy and goes out of his way to help him. In "John Lane's Story," two boys are helped several times by mentors who take a special interest in them. John and Tom become very rich, but their happiness comes not from the money itself but from sharing it with their families.

Fired by wisdom, humor, and imagination, this collection does indeed capture "the lost years." But perhaps more important is the storyteller's ability to remind us of what we have *not* lost--our individual ability to respond to life's challenges with courage and our power to positively affect the lives of others.

--Carla Thomas McClure

A PROMISE KEPT

 I married Joe McGee when I was still fifteen years old and Joe one year older. We both thought we were the luckiest people alive. Our log cabin was new. Joe had cut logs all winter for the cabin. In the spring, a day for a "log rolling" was set. Friends and family came from miles away and built the cabin and a small barn in just one day.

Men, women and children came. The women brought food to cook while the men built the cabin. They brought wedding gifts. Our people gave us some furniture, a cow, a horse and chickens, as well as tools. Late that afternoon a minister married us in our own cabin, not even a few hours old.

Then everyone left, teasing, but wishing us luck. They would travel home—miles away in some cases—maybe camping for the night along the way.

Then Joe and I were alone—alone on a high mountaintop in the Allegheny Mountains west of the Blue Ridge Mountains of Virginia in Pocahontas County, Virginia.

Joe and I went to the highest point above our new cabin to sit on a log to look at the land. We could still hear the sounds of our friends' wagons coming from the deep valleys, along with the far-off sound of their voices echoing through the hills.

We could see in almost every direction from our mountaintop, one blue ridge looking a little higher than the next, with a blue haze around them but deeper blue in the valley. It was a world of forest land with a few dots in the distance that were little farms.

Most people would call this a very lonely land, as no neighbors were within miles. It wasn't lonely to us; it was glorious. We felt that we owned everything as far as we could see. What else was there to want? We had each other and two strong bodies, willing and able to work. We already had a horse, a cow and chickens. With this great start we would use the bountiful forest and work the rich farmland like slaves.

A full moon rose over the mountains to the east, bathing everything in light. Joe loved to play his banjo while we sang together. I suggested that this was a night to play and sing. Joe just said, "We will sing a lot, have many nights to sing, but not tonight." Joe took my hand and gently led me back to the new cabin—our home. There would be a lot of good days ahead and a lot of bad days, but none better than this.

We were up by sunrise. I cooked our first breakfast. We took time to look at what seemed like the whole world from our mountaintop, a beautiful sight. Then it was time to get on with our life's work. As a girl of the mountains I knew all about what had to be done. The very first day meant starting to plow and plant. A chicken house had to be built to protect the chickens. Trees had to be cut and then cut into logs. Then rails were to be split for fences and logs made into pens for the hogs and sheep we would soon need.

I had to gather eggs, milk the cow, churn butter and sew to make clothes. Later, when we had sheep, I would weave cloth for my own clothes. Every day, between my cooking and chores, I would find time to help Joe outside. I loved the long hours of hard work, as did Joe. Everything we did was for us and only us. We almost wished we could delay darkness, as it was interfering with our work time.

Every evening we tried to find time to look at layers of mountain ridges and the ever-changing mountain scenes, but most of all we liked to sit and look at the crops of grain ripening, as well as the growing garden. We never tired of this and loved every minute.

When it rained, we stayed in our cabin. If it was

cold on the high mountaintop, we left a little fire in the fireplace where I cooked. I didn't know how life could get any better than this.

But time and conditions change. We had but few visitors. We welcomed them when they came, but loved every minute of our time together. Joe made trips to the valley for trading and buying things we needed. He also brought newspapers with bad news. It looked like war between the states.

By late summer I knew that I was pregnant. No wonder. Joe teased me that I was just needing more help and decided to raise my own.

Then things got so much worse. The Civil War started. My family and Joe's family lived about ten miles away. Most of the men in the family joined the armies, mostly the Union. Many joined General Lee's Southern Army. The armies were fighting in the valleys where our parents lived. When horses, cows and other livestock began to be taken by both armies, our people left their farms and moved to more remote areas. We were farther away from family help. That summer, one of Joe's brothers was killed in battle. I knew that Joe would join before long.

What was I going to do? Joe checked with both of our families. He wanted to take me to them, even though they were almost worse off than we were. Almost all of the men were in the armies.

I refused to go, assuring Joe that we could deliver our baby. I told him that I had a lot of experience helping my grandmother, a midwife. I stretched the truth about my experience, but I just wasn't about to leave our new home on this beautiful mountaintop.

We passed the summer by working hard. Our gardens and crops grew and grew. We gathered and stored everything, dried beans and fruits. We picked beans and corn. Joe cut hay and made haystacks for the animals for winter.

Then our baby was born. I hadn't had the experience that Joe thought I had, but by following my instructions we got Little Joe into the world, "kicking and screaming." Maybe he knew more about the future than we did.

Then Joe joined the Northern Army, after cutting lots of wood for the winter ahead. I was lonely for Joe.

There was plenty of work—water to carry, animals to be watered and fed, a cow to be milked. Then cooking, washing and feeding the baby. The winter evenings were long, but Joe had taught me to play his banjo before he left. I would play the banjo and sing. Then I started making up songs to sing to Joe during his leave time.

Joe came home several times that winter. He would always find a lot of work to do when at home. In the evenings I would sing and play the banjo, using the songs I had made up. Joe would soon memorize the songs, then play the banjo while we both sang. He would play and sing the songs he was learning in the army.

Joe was now an army scout, as he seemed to have a natural ability to study maps and remember the lay of the land. This gave him a little extra freedom when the armies couldn't move much due to snow and rain.

The bad part of this was that he was free to come home at times when he couldn't work in the fields. Still he was able to plow the garden and fields in the early spring and even help plant part of them. He sometimes was able to help gather the crops.

Mostly, though, it was up to me to make out and make do. We didn't have sheep, so I had no wool to weave, except what Joe could buy. His army pay helped to pay for other necessities.

This was my way of life through the war. Two years after Little Joe was born we had another little boy we named Billy. Joe again was there to help with the delivery.

To me, it seemed the horrible war went on forever. Joe came home and it was glorious. Joe would leave and it was terrible. Even though no words were said, we both knew that we might never see each other again.

4

I missed Joe so much and my family. Three times two of my sisters and a younger brother came to see me. They were afraid to travel for either army would have taken their horses. I lost a brother, killed in service. Joe lost another brother.

I only got news when Joe came home or some distant neighbor came to check on me. Joe's leaves were farther apart now as the fighting was farther away, around Richmond. He came home in January, 1865. He brought more Civil War songs for us to sing. The boys were growing and fun. This leave, like all the others, was much too short and the parting or goodbyes sad as always. Then in the spring a neighbor brought news that the war was over. Now I would wait and watch, watch the road from the valley leading to our mountain home, watching for my Joe to return. The trees were still leafless. I could look a long way into the valley. I could see most of the road all of the way from the valley to our cabin. Every day I watched for Joe.

Even as I worked, I looked for Joe on the road. Surely he would be coming at any hour. Early one morning, I looked and far off in the valley was someone walking. As he got closer, I could see that it was a man. Closer yet, I could see that he was carrying a rifle. This had to be Joe coming home at last, but never returning to war. I felt like yelling and running to meet him. I couldn't leave our little boys who were still in bed.

I waited and waited. As the man came closer, he didn't seem to walk like Joe walked. He looked lankier than Joe, took longer, looser strides. As he neared me, I knew this wasn't Joe. Who is he? My heart dropped. Where is Joe?

He was young, tall and blue-eyed. This was the first time I ever saw Jim Blevins.

Then he asked, "Are you Mrs. McGee?"

I said I was and he said, "I am sorry to have to tell you that your husband, Joe, is dead."

I guess I carried on something awful. I cried and

screamed and pounded my fists on his chest, telling him, "It's a lie. It's a lie."

I don't remember what happened for a long time, being almost out of my mind, except that I kept screaming and hollering and saying, "What will I do? What am I going to do?"

Jim kept saying, "I'm obliged to stay and help you."

When I got my sense back enough to hear what he was saying, I asked, "What do you mean, you are obliged?"

In his soft tome he answered, "I promised a dying man that I would look after you and the boys until you get help."

That's all he told me that night. He slept in the barn. I never thought to ask if he had anything to eat. I reckon I fed my little boys, Joey and Billie, and put them to bed. I know that I laid in my bed and talked to Joe far into the morning, asking what I was to do now and who is this man and why is he here. I got no answers.

The next morning, I wasn't awake until after sun-up, but this man, Jim, was working the small fields. That evening, he brought fresh wild meat already cleaned for cooking. This was our first meat in a long time, and the boys and me ate like we were starved. Jim cooked the meat over an open fire. I just couldn't talk to him yet to ask about Joe, or ask why he was staying.

Again that night, I kept asking Joe, "Why did you leave us? What will we do?" I felt that Joe was telling me to face things, that I had carried through for three years and to talk to this soldier boy and he would tell me. The next day, I went to where Jim was working and asked him why he was here and about that dying man he had made a promise to.

In his soft voice he said, "Ma'am, I'm sorry I have to tell you the story, but it's my duty to tell you."

I just sat and listened, too stunned to move, as he told this terrible tale.

6

He told me that he and Joe were both on scouting duty, one for the North and one for the South, some distance away from the main armies. Jim said he heard a shot and a bullet hit a tree beside him. As he jumped behind a tree, he saw the soldier in blue and returned the shot. The soldier dropped. Jim said when darkness fell, he slipped to near where the soldier had fallen. He heard him moaning and calling for water. Carefully he made his way to him and found the soldier on his back and his rifle to the side. He gave him a drink of water from his canteen. Finding the soldier in blue dying, Jim held his head on his lap and gave him drinks from his canteen. The soldier was Joe. Joe told about his family and made Jim promise to help them as long as he was needed. When Jim rejoined his unit he found the war was over, so he just headed for the mountains to keep his promise.

I was too numb to say much except, "You'll have to leave now. You killed my husband."

Jim only answered, "I'm sorry, ma'am, but I have to keep my promise."

I made my way back to the cabin and talked to Joe long into the night, telling him that the man who shot him just had to leave. I got no answer. The next day I started working in my garden, getting it ready to plant. I never spoke to Jim except to answer his questions about where to find seed to plant. Jim would answer softly, thanking me and always saying "Ma'am."

Every night I would ask Joe what was the right thing to do, telling him that Jim had to leave. I received no answers. Jim kept bringing fresh-killed game and greens from the fields and woods and sleeping in the barn. He cooked on an open fire. I fed the boys what Jim had brought, but I couldn't eat his food for a long time. Jim worked hard and long. It wasn't right for him to have to cook. I still talked to Joe, but got no help, so I just told Jim to eat with us. He was so grateful, but I was determined not to talk to him except when I needed to answer him.

One evening he worked late, planting corn. I fed and put the boys to bed and ate with Jim, not saying anything. Our hands met by accident when we reached for a dish. A shock went through me. I couldn't pull my hand back. It felt so good to have a man's hand in mine after such a long time. Jim apologized, pulling his hand away.

I could still feel Jim's hand on mine long into the night. I talked and talked to Joe, but I got no answer. I found myself causing our hands to touch, feeling a thrill for hours afterward. Then I would ask him to leave again. He would just answer, "I just can't, Ma'am. I promised a dying man."

As much as I talked to Joe I got no help from him.

One evening our hands met and held for a long minute. Jim began to find ways to make our hands meet. One evening Jim put his arm around my shoulder. I had chills for what seemed like hours, except where his arm and hand touched. There it still felt warm.

That night I talked a long time to Joe, saying, "I find it so hard to hate this duty-driven man, especially when he calls our boys, yours and mine, and takes them to the high point above the garden. There he tells them about the flowers, the birds and trees. He shows them the beauty of our high hills and paints our small fields as large woodland. They come back so quiet in awe and wonderment that I sometimes cry. What should I do when we all need him so much?"

I woke while it was still dark. That time I felt that Joe had finally answered, telling me that whatever I decided would be the right decision.

I made up my mind, but I didn't say anything to Jim. That evening I fed the boys early. Then after Jim and I ate without touching hands, he got ready to go back to the barn.

I said, "Jim, I want to talk to you."

He turned, and I asked him, "Do you mean what you said about staying with Joe's family as long as you were needed?"

8

He said, "I'm sorry, ma'am, but a man has to keep his word to a dying man, and I promised that I would stay and help."

Then I told him how I had talked to Joe every night, asking over and over, "How can I keep a man who shot my husband and the boys' father? Yet we need him so much in every way." I continued, "I think Joe answered me last night and told me that whatever I decided would be right. I have decided. Joe's boys and I will need you a long, long time."

Then Jim said, "Even if I had never promised a dying man, I just don't know how I could ever leave you and the boys again."

Then I asked, "Do you think that we should take a trip to the valley tomorrow to find a preacher?"

Jim answered, "That would be the best trip of my life. You and the boys would be mine. Yes, ma'am. That would be the right and proper thing to do."

As he held me in his arms I could only think, "The boys and I will always be taken care of by this duty-driven man."

JOE'S SONG
(MAN OF THE MOUNTAIN)

CHORUS
I'm just a man of the mountain
I'm only a mountain man
Lived all my life on top of these hills
My blood runs through this land

My daddy came to this mountain
When he was just a lad
Mama died when I was a baby boy
This mountain's the only home I've had

I grew up a friend of the forest
I knew the animals and they knew me
I laid awake at night countin' the stars
As I slept under the old oak tree

My daddy died up on this mountain
Left all that he owned to me
I buried him right beside Mama
They sleep together beneath the tall pine tree

I brought my Betty to this mountain
I asked her to be my wife
I promised I'd take good care of her
She said she'd share my mountain life

We had our boys on this mountain
In the cabin that I built by the creek
And as I washed my baby boys
I knew my life was complete

I don't want to leave this mountain
To fight in the valley below
I want to stay here with my family
Buy my country says I gotta go

They wanna make me a soldier
And put me in a suit of blue
But I'd rather stay on my mountain
And taste the morning's new dawn dew

I'm not afraid to defend my country
If I believe what I'm fighting for
But it's brother killing brother
In this blood-thirsty civil war

And Lord knows I'm not a coward
I've never been afraid to fight
But who will play with my children
And hold Betty in the cold dark night?

Well, I guess I better get going
I've waited as long as I can
And even though they call me a soldier
I'll always be just a mountain man.

REPEAT CHORUS

RAINBOW OF SEASONS

I've got a rainbow on my mountain
Got a rainbow for a friend
Got a rainbow when I'm lonesome
Got a rainbow with no end

In the summer I've got sunshine
To keep me warm throughout the day
The clear water of the creek refreshes
As we kick off our shoes and play

The branches of the trees protect us
From the blistering heat of the day
And we picnic in the pine cones
As the summer fades away

In the fall I've got a portrait
Painted by the Master's hand
All the colors of creation
Blend together on His land

Leaves are whispering as they're falling
"See you when the spring is nigh"
They float gently in the soft wind
And lay on the ground to die

When the snow falls there's a mirror
Clear as crystal on the tree
As the sun shines through the branches
God's reflection I can see

Spring comes slowly to the mountain
With the whistling of the wind
Baby buds soon turn to branches
And the hills wake up again

Spring showers reveal the rainbow
Its colorful arch for all to see
The Lord alive in all His Glory
Has revealed Himself to me

CATHERINE'S SONG

"Tell me, lonesome mountains
Answer me, whispering pine
How am I gonna live my life
Without that man of mine?"

How will I raise my baby boys
To grow up like their dad
Why did they take him, wise old owl?
The only man I've ever had.

I don't have much time for grieving
There's just too much work to be done
The children must have food and clothing
And I still need to give them some fun

My heart is heavy from hurting
In my eye there's always a tear
Why did he have to shoot my Joe
Tell me, full moon, if you hear.

This man who's driven by duty
To take care of the children and me
He says he promised the soldier he killed
As he held his head on his knee

Says he made my Joey a promise
Before he slipped into death
That he'd take care of the ones left behind
He said Joe smiled and took his last breath

Oh, bright stars, it's drivin' me crazy
This whole war is killin' us all
The North and the South are being ripped apart
By the blast of that black cannon ball

There's men like my Joe who are dying
And many more that have already gone
Just tell me, oak tree, standing so tall
What do they think they have won?

Death has covered our nation
There's weeping from mothers and wives
Couldn't they just talk at the table
Instead of taking so many young lives?

Oh, night full of stars, can you answer
What do I do with this man
Who has come with the blood of my husband
Shot by the gun in his hand.

And if there's a God up in Heaven
Why did you let it be so?
Why didn't you let this young rebel die
Instead of my dear darlin' Joe?

He was the one with the children
A man I held closer through the night
Oh, whistling wind, if you hear me
How could it ever be right?

Words by Vera Taylor

Music by Mark Tribble

The Story was also made into the following play and shown at the Fayetteville Historical Theatre in Fayetteville, WV. The show was also shown several times in the theatre at the noted Tamarack Arts & Crafts Center in Beckley, WV

Permission will be granted to any amateur group who wishes to produce this play, Please contact:

J. Dennis Deitz
216 Sutherland Dr.
So. Charleston, WV 25303
304-744-2772

There will be no charge by the author, but notification is requested.

A Promise Kept

The Characters

Act One

Catherine Carr McGee: *Married at 15, she is certain that she and Joe together can overcome all obstacles through discipline and hard work We first see her as serious and some what severe in appearance, but our view will change during the play.*

Joseph McGee: At 16, he is a hard-working farmer with a romantic heart. He has a remarkable ability to see what's important and what's not.

The McGee Family: Sally and Tom, Joe's parents
Lewis and Henry, Joe's brothers

The Carr Family: Clara and John, Catherine's parents

Others: *The preacher, friends, a 10-year-old girl and other family members who come for the house-raising and wedding.*

Act Two

Jim: A young confederate soldier with an unusually strong sense of duty and honor.

Joe Junior and Billy: Catherine and Tom's two sons,

Time, Place, and Setting

The events of A Promise Kept take place during the time of the civil war in the Allegheny Mountains of Pocahontas County, Virginia (to become West Virginia).

The set is assembled during the opening scene, a house-raising for Joseph and Catherine. Once assembled, we'll see the inside of a log cabin. a feather bed on one side, a table with chairs near the center of the stage, and a pot-bellied stove next to a sideboard where tin cans of flour. and cornmeal are stored. The backdrop is the cabin's unusually large window, framed by ribbon tied feed sack curtains. The Alleghenies are visible through the window. It is late March, when trees are just beginning to bud.

A Promise Kept - Fayetteville Historical Theatre

ACT ONE

Scene One

Lights up gradually on the nearly bare stage, as though the sun is just rising. Whistling and talking, four men in work clothes and boots enter, carrying wood, nails, and hammers. They begin assembling the table, four chairs, afire place, and a bedframe.

Lewis: You think them lovebirds'll need this fireplace, or you reckon they'll just cling to one another to keep warm?

Tom: Oh, they'll be clingin' alright, but you better bring in some firewood, just the same.

Lewis exits.

Henry: Wish somebody'd build me a cabin like this.

Tom: Find you a woman that'll have you, and we will!

Henry: What they goin' to need four chairs for, way up here on the top of this mountain? Ain't nobody hikin' all this way for dinner,

John: Give me your hammer, Tom. so I can commence on that bed frame.

Two women enter, carrying yards offeed sack meant to be used as curtains. They drop the cloth infront of the picture window and look it over. They are followed by a young girl, about 10, who carries two huge blue tie-back bows.

Sally: What a wonderful view they'll have!

Clara: When you're 15, every view looks wonderful. I wish they were staying closer to us in the valley.

Sally *(puffing her hands on Clara's shoulders)*: Clara, I know it's hard when a daughter marries-

Clara: Catherine is only 15.

Sally *(continues)*: --but my Joe will take good care of her. He's a good man.

Clara: No offense, Sally, but he's only 16. A good boy maybe, but he's not a man yet.

Girl *(interrupting)*:   Can I put the big ribbons on now?

Sally: Not yet.

Sally and Clara drape the curtains over the rod and let them hang down on either side. The curtains should be the most feminine thing in the room

Clara: Of course, I was only 16 when I married Catherine's father. That seems so long ago now.

Sally: Sometimes it seems only yesterday when I married my Tom. Other, times, it doesn't even seem like the same lifetime. I swear, I don't think time moves along evenly.

Clara: Of course it does. It just *seems* faster as we get older.

Sally: Maybe. It's something I want to ask God about after I crossover.

Clara: Ask God?!

Sally: Like my own Mama used to say, He's got a lot of explaining to do. And once I cross that boundary between here and there, I'm hoping he'll be a little freer with the mysteries.

Clara *(taken aback)*:   Well.

Girl: *Now* can I put the big ribbons on?

Sally: Yes, child.

Lewis re-enters, carrying a huge pile of fire wood which he drops as soon as he gets in the door. The wood rolls all over the floor.

Tom: Well, I hope your brother is more careful than you when he carries his bride across that threshold!

Lewis: Aw, Daddy, wood ain't the same thing as a woman.

Henry: Ain't *that* the truth!

The women, finished with the curtains, unfold a double wedding ring quilt and hold it up for inspection.

A Promise Kept - Fayetteville Historical Theatre

Clara: You boys clean up this floor. And bring that feather tick in here so we can spread this quilt on it. The preachers going to be here any minute now.

Sally *(tracing the rings in the quilt, with one hand)*: What God hath joined, let no man put asunder.

There is a bustle on the stage as it is cleared The feather tick is brought in, and the women spread the colorful quilt over it. The preacher arrives, the women call for everyone to take their places, and the wedding party is assembled We see the couple for the first time as they stand before the preacher, whose back is toward the audience.

Catherine's hair is pulled back into a tight but4 and she has flowers in her hair. Joe is wearing a suit. His dark, curly hair might be a little long, but he is very handsome and obviously proud of his bride.

Preacher: Dearly beloved, we gather here in the sight of God to join

in holy matrimony Joseph Allen McGee and Catherine Dora Carr. If anybody knows of any reason these two should not be married, speak now or forever hold your peace.

Catherine's mother, Clara bursts into tears. Sally and others comfort her.

Clara *(to others, In a stage whisper)*: It's just that forever is such a long time.

Sally *(to Clara, also In a stage whisper)*: Not when you're in love, dear. Not when you're in love.

Joe *(turning to his future mother-in-law)*: Mrs. Carr, I'm going to see to it that Catherine here is taken care of for the rest of her life. You got my word on that, Ma'am.

The others nod approvingly.

Preacher: If there are no objections-?

Clara shakes her head no.

Preacher: Well then. Joseph, do you take this woman to be your lawfully wedded wife. to have and to hold, for richer and for poorer. for better and for worse, in sickness and in health. till death do you part?

Joe *(enthusiastically)*: I do for a fact.

Preacher: And do you, Catherine, promise to love, honor, obey, and cherish this man till death do you part?

Catherine: I do.

Preacher: I now pronounce you man and wife.

Henry *(from the back of the crowd)*: Give her a little kiss, Joe, but make it short. I'm hungry!

Laughter as Joe kisses Catherine on the cheek

Sally: There's plenty to eat outside. You all help yourselves.

The crowd moves outside. We can see them passing back and forth outside the large window, talking and carrying plates of food.

Sally: Preacher, can you stay for supper?

Preacher: That's kind of you, Mrs. McGee, but I've got a funeral to preach on the next ridge. Maybe if you could find me a biscuit or two

Sally: Certainly.

Both exit, leaving the room empty. We see the wedding party outside the window. Good-byes are said. We hear the clop of horses feet and the creak of wagon wheels as the guests leave. Joe and Catherine stand together with their backs to the window, waving to Their parting guests. They walk out of view. The outdoor scene changes to a night sky full of stars. All is quiet - except for the night sounds of frogs and crickets. We hear Catherine's voice, but we can't see her yet.

Catherine: I am perfectly capable of walking through a cabin door unassisted.

Joe: Oh, no you don't. It's My sworn duty as a husband to carry you across that threshold.

Catherine: Why, that's the silliest thing I ever- *(shrieks)*

Joe enters the cabin door carring Catherine, who is still kicking her feet –
her shrieks turn to laughter.

Joe (*setting her down, then cupping her face in his hands*): W o m a n ,
what you need is some good kissin'.

Catherine: How do you know what I-

Joe kisses Catherine's forehead, eyelids, cheeks, neck

Catherine (*softly, her eyes closed*): -- need.

A long kiss, finally on the lips.

*As they pull away from one another, Catherine appears to be in a trance.
Her eyes remain closed Joe lets her hair down and we see how very
young she is and how vulnerable.*

Catherine: I am the luckiest girl in Pocahontas County.

Joe: Can't argue with that. Don't see why you'd want to limit it to
this little county, though.

Catherine (*opening her eyes, smiling*); Joe McGee, you don't have an
ounce of humility.

Joe: Oh yes, I do. Come here.

*He takes her to the window, stands behind her with his arms around her
waist as they look outside at the stars.*

Joe: See them stars, the way they move across the sky at night so
slow you don't even notice? And these mountains (*he points*), can't you
feel it? Can't you feel that we belong here, like God brought us here for
some reason? It's like I can feel Him, Catherine, looking directly down at
me, and at you, and I think, "Who am I that God should take notice?"

Catherine: Can you really feel Him?

Joe: Sure. If I'm real quiet, I can almost hear his voice sometimes.
Seems like.

Catherine: Sometimes, when I'm by myself in the woods, and the wind
is blowing, I think it might be Him. Coming to get me. It scares me, Joe.

Joe *(laughing softly)*:   You been listening to too many preachers, Catherine. Too many camp meetings with your mama.

Catherine: Mama-she says My name is too long. She wishes she'd named me Kate.

Joe: No, you're a Catherine all right. Can't think of a prettier name.

Catherine: There's a full moon tonight. *(She turns to Joe)* Why don't we sit on our porch and you can play your banjo and I can sing?

Joe: Oh, we'll sing a lot on this mountain. We'll have many nights to sing songs. But not tonight.

Lights down as they kiss tenderly.

Musical interlude: *(duet, male and female sing a capella-music available:)*

I've got a rainbow on my mountain,
Got a rainbow for a friend
Got a rainbow when I'm lonesome
Got a rainbow with no end.

In the summer I've got sunshine
To keep me worn throughout the day.
The clear water of the creek refreshes
As we kick off our shoes and play.

The branches of the trees protect us
From the blistering heat of the day,
And we picnic in the pine cones
As the summer fades away.

Scene Two

Late August 1861. 7he mountains are visibk through the cabin's large picture window. A tired Catherine, five months pregnant, sits at the table stringing beans.

Catherine: I wish it had rained today so Joe could have stayed in and helped me with these beans.

Joe *(enters cabin carrying another bushel basket of beans)*: Did I hear somebody say green beans?

Catherine *(groaning at the sight)*: I am just tuckered out. I don't know what's wrong with me. Joe stands behind Catherine and massages her shoulders.

Joe: That's what you get for trying to grow your own help.

Catherine *(putting her hands on her stomach)*: Don't you listen to your daddy. I won't let you do a single chore... not till you're three years old, at least.

Joe: It's a shame you can't get' em ready-made. I could sure use some help these next few days. But just look at that field. *(He bounds to the window.)* That'll perk you up for sure. Come on, Catherine, you can see it from here.

Catherine: Why don't you just describe it to me? *(half-sarcastically.)* You have such a way with words.

Joe *(teasing)*: All right, you lazy thing. *(He clears his throat, takes a mock poetic stance.)* I see the late August sun shining down on the year's last cornrows, wide leaves so dark and green they almost look wet. And next to it a field of golden grain-

Catherine: You mean the hayfield?

Joe: As I was saying – the golden grain ripens beneath the golden sun, and we breathe the hours like nectar, till the darkness says we're done.

Catherine *(accusingly)*; You got that from a song.

Joe *(preoccupied, looking out the window as though he sees something)*: The song of life, Catherine, the song of fife. Well, I'll be-

Catherine: What is it?

Joe: Looks like somebody coming around the ridge on horseback.

Catherine: Who?

Joe: It's Lewis!

Joe rushes out the door. Momentarily, through the window, we see him meet Lewis. They talk seriously for a few moments. Catherine continues to sit inside, humming as she strings beans. We can hear them snap. Outside, Joe puts his head in his hands. He has just heard bad news.

Catherine: What is taking them so long? *(She slowly gets up and walks toward the door.)* You all coming in to visit me or you telling secrets?

Joe remains visible through the window, his head still in his hands. Lewis comes to the door.

Lewis: Howdy, Catherine.

Catherine: Lewis, what brings you all the way up here? Lonesome for your little brother?

Lewis: I do miss him. But that's not why I came. *(motions)* Can we sit down?

Catherine: Something's wrong.

Lewis: Yes.

Catherine: What is it?

Lewis *(guiding her to a chair as he speaks, then sitting down at the table himself:* We lost our cattle yesterday. Union soldiers. Said they needed them to feed a new company of men.

Catherine: They can't just --

Lewis: That's what I thought. Till they come. You can't say no to twenty shotguns. And two weeks ago there was a knock on the door and when Mother opened it, six Confederate soldiers raided the house. Took every scrap of metal they could found.

Catherine: Where was Mr. McGee?

Lewis *(surprised)*: Didn't Joe tell you? Daddy joined the Union Army two months ago. So did Henry.-

Catherine *(standing)*: What?!

Lewis *(pauses)*: Then yesterday, another man knocked at the door. *(holding back emotion)* Brought us Henry's things.

Catherine *(dropping back into chair with a sob)*: **No.**

Lewis: Joe always looked up to him so. He took it hard.

Lewis motions toward the window. Catherine turns, sees Joe through the window. Joe drops his hands and slowly walks out of sight.

Lewis *(continues)*: I don't think it's such a good idea for you to stay up here on this mountain all by yourself There's been soldiers coming through every few days now- both sides. Your Mama-

Catherine *(alarmed)*: Is she all right?

Lewis: Your Mama's fine. But she's worried about you being so far away with a baby coming. Mother and me are helping your folks move over to Hatcher's Run. It's a little more out of the way. They thought it might be safer there.

Catherine *(closing her eyes)*: It's all happening so fast. There's just too much to think about.

Lewis: Yes, Ma'am.

Joe enters, walks mechanically to the table.

Catherine: Are you all right?

Joe: They say a man who dies fighting for God is saved for sure.

Lewis: I'm not so sure God has anythin' to do with this war. Brother against brother, father against son There's nothing right about that.

Joe *(suddenly angry)*: Henry didn't give his life for nothing. *(pounds fists on table to accent words)* The Union must stand!

Lewis: What about states' rights? Do you want Mr. Lincoln telling you how to run your farm?

Joe: This ain't exactly a plantation we've got here.

Lewis: It's the principle of the thing.

Joe: Are you saying you're willing to fight for the Confederacy?

Lewis: I'm not saying anything.

Joe: You'd fight for them, when they Idlied our own brother?

A Promise Kept - Fayetteville Historical Theatre

Catherine *(interrupts)*: I hate this war. I hate it.

Lewis *(quietly, after a pause)*: Me too.

Joe *(thoughtfully)*: Boundaries. It's all about boundaries.

Lewis: Well, I heard a rumor out of Wheeling that if they separate Virginia, we'll go with the North. The state of Kanawha or something like that,

Joe: I'm not talking about just state boundaries. I mean the lines you draw between your personal life and your public life. Henry wiped out that boundary when he put his life on the line. So now, he's crossed another boundary, into an unknown country. If he's in the same country as God, we just have to let go and move on and trust that we'll meet him again when we cross over.

Lewis: Brother, you've got more trust than I do.

Joe *(smiling weakly)*: Just the same, I wish he was still here.

Catherine: Well, there's one boundary I'm not going to cross. This war will not make me leave our home.

Joe: Catherine, it might be for the best if you did go to your Mama. With the baby coming this winter, and no one around for miles-

Catherine: What about all that trust in God you were just talking about?

Joe: You're right. Looks like I got an awful little dose of it after all.

Lewis *(rising)*: Listen, I need to ride over to Uncle Albert's before dark. Nobody's been over yet.

Joe *(also rising)*: I'll walk out with you, big brother.

They exit together, talking in low voices about war news. Catherine

Catherine: He's going to go fight. I can feel it. But I'm not afraid. *(trying to convince herself)* I'm not afraid.

Musical interlude: *(solo, female voice, sung a capelia or with a banjo, same tune as previous interlude)*

The few changes necessary for the next scene are made during the interlude.

In the fall I've got a portrait
Painted by the Master's hand
All the colors of creation
Blend together on His land

Leaves are whispering as they're falling
"See you when the spring is nigh."
They float gently in the soft wind
And lay on the ground to die.

Scene Three

Two and a half years later, spring 1864. A dark night sky is visible through cabin window. We hear the sound of a gentle spring rain in the background. A crib and a child's bed have been a&ki4 and set beneath the window. Catherine and Joe have pulled kitchen chairs to the front of the stage, off to one side so that the window is clearly visible to the audience. Joe is paying a banjo (or guitar), and he and Catherine together finish the song begun in the previous two interludes:

When the snow falls there's a mirror
Clear as crystal on the tree
And the sun shines through the branches
God's reflection I can see.

Spring comes slowly to the mountain
With the whistling of the wind
Baby buds soon turn to branches
And the hills wake up again.

Spring showers reveal the rainbow
Its colorful arch for all to see
The Lord alive in all His Glory
Has revealed Himself to me.

Joe: It sure is good to be home, to hear your voice.

Catherine: This past week I've felt Mm I'm living a dream. Joe, is this war ever going to end? It's dragged on for three years now. When will it stop?

28

A Promise Kept - Fayetteville Historical Theatre

Joe: After what happened in Vicksburg and Gettysburg last summer, I don't see how the South has the heart to go on much longer.

Catherine: When are you coming home for good?

Joe: I'd give anything to just stay here with you and not go back.

Catherine: Good! Why don't you do that?

Joe: You know I couldn't desert now. There ain't very many scouts trained the way my Daddy trained me. A lot of men's lives have been saved because of that.

Catherine: You always were good at studying maps and remembering the lay of the land. And your hearing is so keen. I know you're a good scout.

Joe: Correction: My hearing used to be keen. Baby Billy screamed so loud after he was born I thought my ears would never stop ringing.

Catherine *(sighs)***:** Maybe he knew what kind of world he was coming into.

Joe: look at them Catherine. Look at what you and me made. They're beautiful boys. God will watch after them.

Catherine: Do you remember the day we were married I told you that sometimes I felt like God was coming after me? Through the woods? *(pause, Joe nods)* I don't feel that way anymore. Sometimes I can feel him near me, and it doesn't scare me at all.

Joe: I'm glad. Just look at everything he's given us two strong bodies to work the land, these mountains for a home, this rain so the crops will grow, our boys--each other. We're mighty lucky, Catherine,

Catherine: Teach me another war song, Joe, so I can sing it after you go back. I can imagine I might be singing it with you even though we're miles apart.

Joe *(strumming his banjo as he talk)***:** Sometimes at night when the whole valley is filled with camp fires, it looks like the stars have fallen out of the sky. Tiny flickering lights all over the place. Then one group of men will start to sing, then another joins in, then another, till soon the

29

whole valley is filled with one voice beneath the stars. Almost like a prayer.

As Joe sings the first verse, and the chorus of "The Yellow Rose of Texas," Catherine closes her eyes to listen. After he sings a couple lines, a man dressed in the blue colors of the Union stands up outside the window. He is holding a lighted candle, and joins in with Joe's singing. With the next line, another man stands up, then others, one at a time, joining in Joe's song one by one till they all finish together, their candles flickering like individual campfires.

There's a yellow rose in Texas
I'm going there to see,
No other cowboy knows her,
Nobody only me.

She cried so when I left her,
It liked to broke her heart.
And if we never meet again
We nevermore shall part.

CHORUS

She's the sweetest rose of color
this cowboy ever knew.
Her eyes are bright as diamonds.
they sparkle like the dew.

You may talk about your dearest maids
And sing of Rosie Lee,
But the yellow rose of Texas
Beats the belles of Tennessee.

Catherine: I can almost hear your army buddies singing with you.

Joe: They're never far away anymore, especially the ones that got killed. They stay with you.

Catherine: Whatever happened to John, the fellow from Phillipi that you liked so much? Did he ever hear from his fiancee?

Joe: They carried him home last month. Lost both legs, but it looked like he might make it.

Catherine: So much pain and loss. I don't see how this nation can stand it much longer. Every family we know has lost someone to the war.

Joe: It's for a reason, Catherine. You've got to believe that. Henry and Lewis and your brother Breec – they gave their lives for something bigger than all of us.

Catherine: Joe, I've carried two lives inside me now. I've seen how helpless they come into the world, how sweet they are, fresh from heaven. I know how hard I've worked to keep them healthy. There is no reason. No reason strong enough to get me to send them out to a battlefield.

Joe *(sighs)***:**   Sometimes I think you're right.

We hear the baby begin to cry. Catherine goes to his crib and picks him up. She never notices the soldiers.

Catherine: I believe someone is hungry. Shhh, don't you wake your brother.

She sits on the bed and begins to unbutton the front of her dress. Covering herse4fwith a cloth, she nurses the baby. Joe pulls his chair around so that he can see her as he sings:

Song: "Man of the Mountains" *(music available)*

I'm just a man of the mountain,
I'm only a mountain
Lived all my life on top of these hills,
My blood runs through this land.

I brought my Catherine to this mountain.
I asked her to be my wife.
I promised I'd take good care of her
She said she'd share my mountain life.

We had our two boys on this mountain,
In the cabin that we built by the creek.
And as I washed My baby boys,
I knew my life was complete.

A Promise Kept - Fayetteville Historical Theatre

I don't want to leave this mountain
To fight in the valley below.
I want to stay here with my family,
But my country says I gotta go.

They wanna make me a soldier
And put me in a suit of blue.
But I'd rather stay on my mountain'
And taste the morning's new dawn dew.

I'm not afraid to defend my country-
I believe in what I'm fighting for.
But it's brother against brother
In this blood-thirsty civil war.

And Lord knows I'm not a coward
I've never been afraid to fight.
But who will play with my children
And hold Catherine in the cold, dark night?

Men in uniform, still standing outside the window, join Joe for the last verse:

I'm just a man of the mountain,
My blood runs through this land.
Although they may call me a soldier,
In my heart I know I'm just a mountain man.

Lights down.

ACT TWO

Scene One

May 1865. A very bright, sunny morning shines through the window, with the mountains visible. 7Vs is the brightest the set has looked since the day she and Joe were married. Catherine is sweeping the wooden floor of the cabin, stopping every few seconds to look out the door or the window. Two boys, ages three and two, sleep in one small bed at the foot of the large bed.

Catherine *(after looking out the window yet again)*: Boys, I don't know what is keeping your father. Over a month now since the fighting stopped, and he's still not home. I wonder how long it takes to walk from Richmond? Oh well, no matter. He could be here any hour now, any minute. *(goes to window again, hangs out)* Wait a minute. I think I see someone, far off in the distance. That could be Joe!

Excitedly, she puts her broom down and starts to run out the front door, but stops short. turns to look at the children.

Catherine: No, I can't leave you sleepyheads here alone. We'll just wait. *(She resumes sweeping, but immediately goes to look out the window again.)* It's definitely a man. I'm glad I baked fresh biscuits this morning. *(looks again)* He's carrying a rifle. That's got to be Joe. *(She puts her broom down again goes over to the sideboard next to the pot-bellied stove, and starts peeling potatoes. Her face is toward the audience, and she seems to be speaking to them)* I'll have him a real welcome home breakfast. Biscuits, fried potatoes, eggs. I wonder if I've got a few apples in the cellar. I think I'm more nervous that I was on our wedding day! This is going to be the best day of my life.

A knock at the door, which is open. A smile spreads across Catherine's face.

Catherine: You can't trick me. Joe McGee!

Man's voice: Mrs. McGee?

Catherine's smile drops.

Man's voice: Excuse me, Ma'am. Are you Mrs. McGee?

A Promise Kept - Fayetteville Historical Theatre

Catherine turns slowly to the door and looks at the stranger, who is visible in the door way.

Catherine: Yes, I am. But you're not Joe.

Man: No, Ma'am. My name is Jim. Jim Blevins. I'm sorry to have to tell you this, Ma'am, but

Catherine *(realizing why he has come)*: No.

Jim: I'm awful sorry, Ma'am, but your husband Joe-he's dead.

Catherine: No. It's a he. It's a lie! It's not true! It's a lie!

As she says this, Jim enters the cabin to try to comfort her. -She beats her fists against his chest as she repeats the words over and over. Jim tries to calm her down.

Jim: I know it's hard, Ma'am. I'm sorry.

She is almost out of her mind with grief. He guides her to the bed and helps her lie down, where she curls into a fetal position, her back toward the room.

Catherine: What'll I do? What'll I do? What will I ever do?

The boys have woke up and begin to cry Catherine is too grief-stricken to notice. She continues to cry silently, though occasionally we hear her sob or repeat a phrase.

(If children are available that can handle the parts of Joe Junior and Billy, even if they're slightly older than the time line would allow, use them in the scene. If not, use recorded or offstage children's voices and let Jim pantomime his interaction with the boys.)

Jim *(glancing worriedly at Catherine, bat going to the foot of her bed to squat down next to the boys)*: I don't think I've ever seen two more handsome-looking boys. You must be Joe Junior. And you must be Billy.

Joe Junior: Are you our daddy?

Jim: No, boys, I'm not. But I knew your daddy. In fact, he sent me here to help take care of you.

Joe Junior: Why?

Jim: He - can't came home right now, see.

Joe Junior: Why?

Jim *(with obvious difficulty)***:** He'd love to be here with you right now, but he had to go somewhere. That's why he sent me.

Billy: I hun-gwy,

Jim: I'll fix you some breakfast. *(Looks around sees biscuits on sideboard. He finds a jar of jam and brings the biscuits to the table, begins to spread jam on them)*

Joe Junior: I want Mommy to fix it.

Jim: She can't right now, Joe Junior.

Joe Junior: Why?

Jim: Your mommy doesn't feel good this morning. We hear Catherine sob,

Billy: Mommy cries.

Joe Junior: Why does Mommy cry?

Jim *(patiently)***:** Now listen here. Your Mommy is going to be just fine, don't you worry. But she hurts right now. We have to take cam of her. Can you help me do that?

Billy: Help Mommy.

Jim: That's right.

Joe Junior: Where does Mommy hurt?

Jim: Here, do you like blackberry jam on your biscuits?

Joe Junior: Yes, Mister. Where does she hurt?

Jim: It's her heart that's hurting. Her heart. *(pause)* Eat your biscuits and I'll take you boys for a walk.

Billy: Mommy's heart hurt.

John: Your Mommy's going to stay here and rest.

Billy: Mommy rest.

Jim picks up Billy, Joe Junior walks beside him They exit the cabin. The scene outside the window changes to night. Jim brings the already asleep boys back inside and puts them to bed. He stands a few feet from Catherine and addresses her. Her face is still turned toward the wall. She hasn't moved.

John: You ought to eat something, Ma'am. Me and the boys got a rabbit today. I left some for you on the sideboard.

Joe: Talk to him, Catherine. He has something important to tell you.

Catherine *(giving no sign that she hears Joe's voice)*: You'd tell me what to do if you were here. I wish you were here with me, Joe.

Joe steps through the window and stands over Catherine.

Joe: You've got to face things, Catherine. You carried through for three years with me gone most of the time. You can do this thing.

Catherine: I don't know if I can be strong any more. Yesterday morning, when I thought I saw you walking home, my heart was singing. It won't ever sing again, Joe.

Joe: Catherine, talk to this soldier boy. Jim. He'll help you.

Catherine: I feel like I can almost hear your voice. Joe. Like you're so close I could reach out and touch you-

She sits up in bed, stretches one arm out toward the spot where Joe stands. He also extends one arm. Their fingers are just inches apart.

Jim appears in the door way. Joe backs away and sits on a small stool beside the bed, looking down at the floor.

Jim: I heard you calling.

Catherine: I wasn't calling for you.

Jim *(turning to go)*; Sorry to bother you, Ma'am.

Joe *(whispers)*: Talk to him. Catherine. Talk to him.

Catherine: Wait. *(He tarns, she sues out of bed and sits at the table* I need to ask you something.

Jim comes back in and sits across the table from her.

A Promise Kept - Fayetteville Historical Theatre

Catherine: About Joe. I feel like I need to ask you about Joe.

Jim: Yes, Ma'am. I'm sorry I have to tell you the story, but its my duty to tell you.

Catherine listens, not moving, as he tells his tale.

Jim: Me and Joe were both scouts, Ma'am. Only he was for the North, and I was for the South. We were some distance away from the main armies. Everything was so still, I didn't think nobody was around for miles. Then I heard a rifle shot, and a buffet hit the oak tree just beside me. I saw a soldier in blue uniform and returned fire. The soldier dropped. I waited. I didn't know whether anyone else might have been around and heard the rifle shots. When it got dark, I slipped over to where the soldier had fallen. I heard him moaning and calling for water. I was careful, g it might be a trick. but when I found him on his back with his rifle out to the side, I saw that he was dying. I gave him a drink of water from his canteen. He looked about 20, the same age as me. I couldn't let him die alone. I held his head in my lap and kept giving him water when he asked for it. He told me his name was Joe McGee.

Catherine breathes in sharply but says nothing.

He told me about his family. He made me promise to come and find you and help you as long as you needed. He told me how to find his place. I made him a promise, Ma'am. When I went back to the unit I found the war was over, so I headed for these mountains to keep my promise. I'm not one to go back on my word. Ma'am.

Catherine *(in a flat tone)*: You'll have to leave now. You killed my husband.

Jim: I'm sorry, Ma'am, but I have to keep my promise.

Catherine gets up and walks mechanically back to the bed, passing Joe- still seated on the stool- as she does.

Joe *(without looking up)*: Listen to him. Catherine.

Catherine: You killed my Joe. You'll have to leave.

A Promise Kept - Fayetteville Historical Theatre

Jim: I need to get some com planted tomorrow, Ma'am so you and the boys will have something to eat this summer. I'm sorry, Ma'am. It's my duty.

Jim exits, Catherine is curled up in bed. facing the wall again. Joe walks over to her.

Joe: You've got to accept this thing, Catherine.

Catherine *(wails)*: Noooo! I won't accept this, I won't, I won't.

Song: *This song should be sung a capella by a clear, mournful female voice. (Music available.)*

Tell me, lonesome mountains,
Answer me, whispering pine-
How am I gonna live my life
Without that man of mine?

How will I raise my baby boys
To grow up like their dad?
Why did they take him, wise old owl?
The only man I've ever had.

My heart is heavy from hurting,
In my eye there's always a tear.
Why did he have to shoot my Joe?
Tell me, full moon. if you hear.

This man who's driven by duty
To take care of the children and me,
He says he promised the soldier he killed
As he held his head on his knee.

Says he made my Joey a promise
Before he slipped into death,
That he'd take care of the ones left behind,
He said Joe smiled and took his last breath.

Oh, bright stars, it's driving me crazy,
This war is still killing us all-
The North and South weren't the only things
Ripped apart by that black cannon ball,

38

If there's a God up in Heaven
Why did you let it be so?
Why didn't you let this young rebel die
Instead of my dear darling Joe?

Oh, night full of stars, can you answer
What do I do with this man,
Who has come with the blood of my husband
Shot by the gun in his hand.

Scene Two

Four months later. A sunny day in early September 1865. Catherine is seated in a new rocking chair in front of the picture window, Her hair is pulled back into a somewhat severe bun. She is piecing a colorful quilt top-a flower garden pattern. We hear Jim's and the children's voices outside, but we don't see them.

Children's laughter.

Jim: All right, enough storytelling for today. We've got some fish to catch.

Joe Junior: Can I catch the biggest one today, Jim?

Jim: You can if you're the best fisherman.

Billy: I want a big fish. too.

Jim: They don't stand a chance against the three of us. *(We see Jim walk past the window and knock on the front door before stepping inside.)* I was wondering, Ma'am, didn't you say you had some extra fish hooks somewhere?

Catherine *(rising)*: In a matchbox on the mantle-

They both start toward the fireplace and reach for the match box at the same time. Their hands touch, and Jim puts his on top of Catherine's. Neither one moves.

Jim: You mean this matchbox, Ma'am?

Catherine *(making no move to pull her hand away)*:   Yes.

They stand for a few moments looking at one another as though hungry yet uncertain.

Joe Junior *(his face appears in the window)*:   Hurry, Jim. All the good ones will be gone.

Jim *(loud enough for Joe junior to hear, but still looking at Catherine)*:   Don't you worry. We won't let that happen.

Gently, he takes his hand from Catherine's, picks up the matchbox and takes out three hooks. He offers the box back to Catherine. who passes her hands over his before taking the box- Quickly she looks down at the floor as though embarrassed Jim touches her shoulder before he turns to leave.

Billy's face pops up beside Joe Junior's in the window.

Joe Junior: Look what I made!

Billy: Mommy's heart hurt.

Jim takes the biscuits and fried apples out to the porch, then comes back in and gets his rifle before walking back out the door.

Jim: It looks like you boys like my fried apples'

Joe Junior: They're Grandpa's apples. He grows big apple trees where he lives.

Jim: Is that right?

Joe Junior: Uh-huh.

Jim: Mrs. McGee. I'll be back this evening. I'm going to see about getting those fields plowed.

No response, We see Jim walk past the window. After a moment, Catherine walks back into the house and lies down on the bed again.

Catherine: You boys stay there on the porch where I can keep an eye on you, all right?

Joe Junior: We will, Mommy.

Billy: Mommy sick.

A Promise Kept - Fayetteville Historical Theatre

Catherine's hands are clasped as in prayer.

Catherine: What'll we do. Joe? What'll we do without you?

She drifts in and out of consciousness as the light begins to dim toward evening. The sky outside turns to night again. Jim returns and puts the boys to bed.

Jim: I'll be in the bam if you need anything tonight, Ma'am. You should know I'm obligated to stay. It's my duty.

He exits.

Catherine: Joe, why did you leave us? What will we do. You know I was never very good at prayer. Talk to me, Joe.

Outside the window, Joe stands up, once again in his Union uniform holding a candle.

Catherine: I felt like that man had something to tell me, Joe, but I just couldn't talk to him about you, Joe. I don't even know him.

No response.

Jim: I'm obliged to stay and help you. I promised a dying man that I'd look after you and the boys till you got help.

Still no response.

Jim: I'll be sleeping in the barnif you need anythin', Ma'am.

Jim exits.

Catherine *(turning onto her back her hands clasped as in prayer)*:
Joe, what am I going to do now? Won't you talk to me. Joe? Tell me what to do. I just can't go on. I just can't do it. God won't answer my prayers. He doesn't understand me like you, Joe. Tell me what to do. *(She sobs herself to sleep)*

Outside the window, Joe stands up. He is wearing his Union uniform and carries a candle. A gunshot wound is visible in his side. He moves his lips but we can't hear any sound.

He lowers himself out of sight as another morning dawns, just as bright as the previous day. Jim is peeling apples. The boys are not in sight. Catherine awakes with a start, sitting upright in the bed

Catherine: The sun came up.

Jim: Yes, Ma'am.

Catherine *(to herself)*: I didn't think it would. I didn't think the sun could shine again. *(Suddenly aware that the boys aren't in their beds)* The boys-

Jim: Sitting on the porch, Ma'am – playing with your wooden spools. I can see them from over here, Ma'am. I hope you don't mind about the spools.

Catherine puts her feet on the floor. sits up on the bed.

Jim: You better eat something, Ma'am. If you're able. The boys need you. I took them out with me yesterday, but I need to get started in those fields today.

Catherine doesn't answer, but gets up and walks slowly out to the porch. We hear her and the boys but don't see them Jim continues to prepare their breakfast. We hear the sound of apples frying.

Billy: Mommy better?

Billy: Mommy, I catch fish for you.

Joe Junior: Me too, Mommy.

Catherine: You boys be careful and mind – Stops short of saying Jim's name)

Their faces disappear from view. Catherine looks at the hand Jim had touched, passes her other hand over it as though trying to feel his touch again.

Catherine: They grow so fast, Joe, I wish you could be here to see how they've grown. *(She, goes back to the rocking chair pulls the quilt top onto her lap, and watches as she stitches the pieces together.)* They're awful fond of Jim. *(Pause)* I don't know what to do about him, Joe. I've told him every day for four months to leave. But he just says the same thing: "I just can't Ma'am. I'm obliged to stay on account of the promise I made." Nearly every day he brings fish or fresh killed game. He was cooking on an open fire by the smokehouse and eating his meals out there until I took pity on him and told him he may as well eat with us at the table. *(pauses, looks around as though she expects a response)* Did you hear that. Joe? I took pity on the man that killed you. I don't know what's wrong with me. (pause) He seemed grateful. (pause) Still, I didn't talk to him except when I needed to answer him. Catherine stops sewing, sits still for a moment, gets out of her chair, and impatiently throws the quilt top to the floor. Its colors spread.

Catherine: Joe McGee, you're not one bit of help! I've talked to you all summer and you haven't given me an answer yet. What am I supposed to do about this man?

She paces back and forth across the floor as she speaks.

Catherine: Something happened a few weeks ago, Joe. Jim worked late in the fields. I fed the boys and put them to bed and ate, with Jim, not saying anything. Then *(she stops pacing)* our hands met-by accident-when we both reached for the same dish. A shock went through me. *(She rubs one hand with the other)* It-it just felt so good to have a man's hand in mine after such a long time. *(She drops her hands, begins pacing again.)* Jim apologized and pulled his hand away. But I could feel it for hours after that, long into the night. What do you think of that. Joe?

She stops and looks around the room as though she expects Joe to appear. When he doesn't, she resumes.

After that, I found myself causing our hands to touch more often. I couldn't help it, Joe. I just needed to touch something solid, something real. Afterward, I would ask him to leave again. He always answered the same thing: "I just can't Ma'am. I made a promise."

She pauses again.

Last Sunday evening I was reading my Bible and thinking about you and just started crying, right there in front of the boys and Jim. He didn't say a word. He just came over and put one hand on my shoulder and left it there till I got hold of myself That night turned cool and I chilled in our big old lonely hilled all over, except for where Jim had touched. There it still felt warm. What I'm trying to say, Joe, is-I'm having a hard time hating this duty-driven man. You've got to give me an answer soon.

She falls to her knees on the quilt top next to the rocking chair, assuming an attitude something like prayer. Her hair loosens and falls down around her face. Her voice becomes more quiet and pleading.

He calls our boys, Joe, yours and mine, and takes them to the high point above the garden. Tells them the names of flowers, birds, trees. He shows them the beauty of our mountain and paints our small field as a large woodland clearing. They come back so quiet in awe and wonderment that sometimes I cry. I love you Joe. I always will. But I can't go on hating this man that killed you. What should I do when we **all need him so much?**

She rests her head in the seat of the rocking chair. We hear her muffled question:

What should I do, Joe?

Joe appears again in the window. He is still in his Union uniform

Joe: I can't help you any more, Catherine. I've got to go on. I don't know how to make you hear me.

Catherine *(momentarily lifts her head from the chair)*: How do I make you hear me, Joe?

Joe *(steps into the room, puts his hand on Catherine Is head)*: I h e a r you, Catherine. And I think you've been hearing me too. You just can't accept my answer. You just can't accept that I've crossed a boundary to where I can't come back. But the veil between us isn't that solid. You can hear me if you let yourself. Catherine.

Catherine *(slowly lifts her head again looks around almost whispers)*: Joe, is that you?

Now that he finally has her attention. Joe kneels on the floor beside his wife and puts his hands on hers, and whispers into her ear.

Joe: Forgive him, Catherine, as I have. Then whatever you decide will be right.

A Promise Kept - Fayetteville Historical Theatre

Catherine *(standing up, looking all about her)*: I hear your voice, Joe!

Joe *(again):* Whatever you' decide will be right.

Catherine *(almost in tears):* I love you. Joe.

Joe: Remember, whatever you decide will be right. *(he exits)*

Catherine falls back into the rocking chair, her eyes full of tears. She pulls the half-finished quilt top over her lap but doesn't resume work on it. She is still sitting that way when Jim and the boys come back from the river. We hear their voices before we see them.

Joe Junior: My fish is so big I bet it even tastes big! *(breaks into a run passes the window, enters the cabin door.)* Mommy, I caught the biggest fish! - Look! *(He holds up a large, dripping bass.)*

Catherine *(comes out of her reverie):* Joe Junior, get that thing outside-you're dripping on my new quilt top!

He runs back out the door.

Jim *(sticks his head through the window):* Sorry, Ma'am. *(Walks around to front door, enters, and gets a skillet from on top the stove)* We'll have you a mess of fish fried up in no time. *(He goes out and comes back in a few seconds later with a large plate offish.)* Come on. boys! Let's see how your Mama likes these fish you caught her. All sit at the table. All watch Catherine take the first bite.

Joe Junior: Is it good, Mommy?

Catherine: I don't think I've ever had a better bass, Joe Junior. Did you catch this all by yourself?

Joe Junior: Uh-huh. *(He bites into apiece himself It tastes big!*

Billy: Mommy happy?

Catherine: Yes, baby.

Billy: Mommy's heart not hurt anymore.

Catherine (smoothing back Billy's hair): Mommy-forgives. *(She doesn't look at Jim but he looks up at her and stops eating.)*

Joe Junior: What's that?

45

Catherine: It's what you do to make your heart stop hurting. *(presses her lips together)* Why don't you boys take your plates and go eat on the front porch. It's such a nice evening. *(watches as they go out the door, looks down at her plate)* I need to talk to you,

Jim: Yes, Ma'am.

Catherine *(looking directly into his eyes for the first time)***:** D o   y o u mean what you say about staying with Joe's family as long as you're needed?

Jim: I'm sorry, Ma'am, but a man has to keep his word to a dying man, and I promised that I would stay and help.

Catherine gets up and walks to the window, her back to Jim. She speaks haltingly at first but her words assume a more urgent tone as she goes on.

Catherine: I've talked to Joe every night since you came, asking over and over what I should do, how I could possibly keep the man who shot him and took our boys' father away. *(pause)* Lately I've relized how much we need you – the boys *(pause, she turns toward him but looks at the floor)* and me -in every way. *(She walks closer to Jim her words increase in urgency.)* When I talked to Joe today, I got an answer. It was as clear as if he was standing right next to me. He said-he forgives you, and I should too. Then he said whatever I decided would be right. *(She sits next to Jim and places both her hands on Jim's.)* I have decided that Joe's boys and I will need you for a long, long time.

Jim *(taking her hands as though to warm them)***:**   I'm awful glad to hear you say that, Ma'am. Even if I hadn't made that promise, I just don't know how I could ever leave you and the boys. I know I don't deserve none of you, I know it's my fault your Joe is gone,

Catherine *(tiredly)***:**   It's the war's fault, Jim.

Jim *(looks up)***:** I believe that's the first time I ever heard you call me by name.

Catherine: Do you think we should take a trip to the valley tomorrow and find a preacher?

A Promise Kept - Fayetteville Historical Theatre

Jim: That would be the best trip of my life. Yes, Ma'am. Then you and the boys would be mine. *(Hastens to add)* It's more than I deserve, but I'd take care of you and the boys. Just like I promised. Because I want to.

Catherine: If there's one thing I'll never question, Jim, its your sense of duty and honor. I know me and the boys would always be taken care of.

Jim: We'll find that preacher right away, Ma'am. That would be the right and proper thing to do.

Catherine *(amused)***:** Do you think you can call me Catherine?

Jim: Yes, Ma'am. *(He smiles)* Catherine.

Catherine: Good. *(She touches his cheek with her hand)* Because the rest of my life might be a long time to be called Ma'am.

THE RESCUE—PART ONE
Tom's Story

 For two days I had been alone on the trail of the Indians who had raided the settlement that spring, killed some of the settlers, burned cabins and taken a prisoner, Molly Preston. Why Molly had not been killed I could only guess. Maybe she was needed to help carry the stolen loot from the cabins.

A rescue party had been organized, with Hawk Hayes heading the party. I joined the rescue party, and for three days we followed the Indians' trail. After a day or so the raiders split into three groups. The rescue party quarreled over which trail to follow before deciding on one of the three trails. That's where I left them. I had scouted all three trails, and they were not following the group which had Molly.

When I told them how I knew which group Molly was with, they acted as if I was an ignorant kid, especially Jake Clay, a nineteen-year-old fellow who planned to marry Molly. Jake was a big, burly fellow who sneered at my ideas.

Most of the rescue party considered me as useless in the rescue attempt. They would have all laughed if they had known that I planned to marry Molly. I was barely sixteen years old, six foot two inches tall and rawboned, but not filled out yet. I was the youngest of my family and was considered lazy and useless in the clearing of land and farming. I was gone much of the time hunting, but I did bring home a lot of game and furs which were badly needed by the family, so my wanderings were tolerated.

My parents only allowed me to go to the wild backwoods because they knew that I would camp and hunt with old Ed Luther, who had spent most of his life hunting in Indian country and had even lived with the Indians. Ed liked to have me along, even when I was only thirteen, young, skinny and agile, while Ed was old and crippled. I spent weeks with him while he taught me woods lore and the ways of the Indians.

Ed almost seemed to smell out Indian war parties and would warn the settlers. He usually camped in an area between the settlements and Indian country.

I never realized how much Ed had taught me until I was out a day with the rescue party. They were frontiersmen, but I soon knew that I was reading from their signs and camps things that the rescue party wasn't seeing. I was disgusted. How could they fail to see things that were so clear to me, things Ed had taught me? These men were more farmers and settlers than frontiersmen, but they were good at defending their settlements.

When I would try to explain what I was seeing, the men in the rescue party would laugh, especially Jake. I had grown seven or eight inches in the last year, but I was considered useless by these hard-working people. They didn't know how much time I had spent with Ed or how much he had taught me.

Jake didn't like it that I often talked with Molly when I was at home. Even though he didn't think she would take me seriously as long as he was available, he still didn't want to see me around her.

I knew Molly still thought of me as a young boy she liked, but she would listen to me talk of the woods, the birds and the wild animals. I told her about the things Ed had talked with me about and how to survive in the wilderness. She often had said that she would live like I lived had she been born a boy. I told her his stories of how women captives had survived and left signs to be followed in case rescuers followed. Molly loved these stories and would listen for hours. I kept telling her these things so that I could be around her.

When we started following the Indian raiders I watched carefully for signs Molly might leave. The first thing I saw was an occasional heel print. The Indians were careless at first, only trying to get away fast and not caring if they left a trail. Molly sometimes found a soft spot in the trail and put her full weight on one heel, leaving a deep imprint.

When the war party split into three groups, which would Molly be with? At this point they would cover up their trails more carefully or try to walk on harder ground. I followed all three trails until I found two more heel prints, but they were far down one of the covered trails. When I reported these findings to the rescue party, they laughed at me, saying that it was just one of the Indians. Jake was especially scornful, but I did notice that the deeper we went into the woods the quieter Jake seemed to get. No longer could he whip the whole war party by himself.

I announced that I was going to follow what had to be Molly's trail by myself. I had everything I needed: rifle, balls and powder. Jake called me a "babe in the woods," but they could hardly stop me. Later I learned that the rescue party had turned back two days later, not having a person in the group who was well trained to follow a trail.

I was on my own in Indian country and woods I had never seen before. I more or less knew the lay of the land, remembering what Ed and others who had been there had told me.

The waters of the New River and the Sandy would be flowing mostly north, along with the rivers of Kentucky. Kentucky had many settlements by this time, so the war party would probably be from the Indian villages in the Ohio country.

The three parties of raiders would likely meet near where the Sandy River emptied into the Ohio.

More than likely I could get to that point before any of the war parties, but I might lose the trail of the party Molly was with, for there might be a lot of other Indian raiders or hunters in this area, and I would not know one from the other. I just had to follow the trail of the raiders who had Molly with them. This was dangerous as Ed had told me they always had a brave or two watching the back trail, at least for awhile. I just had to follow the trail for awhile until I could get the general direction of their goal. I figured that I could find some clue other than Molly's heel prints. Her captors would be watching her more carefully and would make their path in higher and harder ground.

After another day I found faint signs of where they had camped. Here I found where two small branches had been broken from a limb and were still hanging. I was sure this was Molly's sign.

A day or two later I found another faint campsite and two more small broken branches still hanging. Molly must have broken them during the night. By this time I could follow the general direction they were following, an old buffalo trail. This way I was able to leave the trail much of the day and find it again before dark.

For food I had berries and nuts, and I set small snares at night for small game. Sometimes I could kill game with a little bow and arrow Ed had taught me to make.

Now when I found their old campsites I could no longer find broken branches. Molly's captors must have caught on to this. I carefully raked the leaves from the campfire site. Molly now seemed to have the job of digging a hole for the fire. The fire would be put out the next morning by putting dirt back and covering the sit with leaves.

In one of the places where they had camped I found that she had put the letter "M" in the soft dirt. I hoped she wouldn't do this often as her captors would see her making the letter. She must have known the danger and would only do so when not watched.

I followed the trail to the mouth of the Sandy where it emptied into the Ohio River. There was a campsite where the three groups of raiders must have agreed to meet at the time they first separated. The other two groups must have gotten there first since the signs of Molly's group were only a day or two ahead of me, if I had read their signs right.

Carefully I uncovered the remains of the campfire. Under the leaves, the dirt over the ashes had been packed down hard. Molly always left it a little loose. The larger group had for some reason taken this job away from her. Maybe they had captured another prisoner or had caught her leaving marks in the soft dirt. I started looking more carefully now, knowing that she was apt to leave some other sign. I finally found a sign on the bark of a small tree where she must have been tied up. She must have wiggled back and forth until whatever she had been bound with had made marks in the bark of the tree. If this was done for some purpose, what was the purpose? I carefully removed the leaves on the campfire side where they would have tied her. Then I saw a small mark on the ground in the shape of an arrow pointing almost north. How she knew what direction they planned to go or how she managed to make the mark while bound up I didn't know. I knew, though, that the Indians were going to have trouble holding that prisoner if they let her learn how to survive in this wild land.

After dark I could see the stars, and the arrow pointed a few degrees west of the North Star. I knew that I could follow the direction they were taking her, if not to the exact village. From what Ed had told me, this would be near the Chillicothe Indian lands, and maybe the big village. I hoped it wouldn't be near the large villages.

I floated and swam across the Ohio, using my

tomahawk to cut off one end of a small dead log to use for support.

This was Indian country. There were signs of other raiding or hunting parties. I finally found one trail that seemed to go more nearly in the direction Molly's arrow had pointed. Would Molly still leave any signs? She would know that no rescue party would dare follow into this wild Indian land. The Indians would be less careful, knowing the same thing. Still, I followed, but very carefully, not knowing when I would run into an Indian hunting party. Molly would surely think that it would be useless to still leave clues. If so, who would the clues be left to guide? She would think no one in our settlement would be experienced and capable of surviving in Indian territory.

I didn't think that she would believe her boyfriend, Jake, would know enough to survive. That left me. Molly was sixteen and had matured early, while I had grown up late. I was sure that she felt, like most of our neighbors, that I was a fairly useless young boy. Maybe she was only being kind to me and meant nothing more. She didn't know that I hoped to marry her. Yet she knew that I knew the woods and had absorbed much about Indian ways from Ed. Even though I was barely sixteen, if she left any more signs, the signs would be for me, Tom Wilson.

After following the trail for three days I found another sign. Someone was using a short, sharp stick as a cane. Was it Molly, or had a short Indian hurt an ankle and was using the stick for a cane? Her captors would probably pay no attention to her using a cane if she pretended to be slightly lame. They would never dream anyone would be following them into the heart of Indian country with hunting parties everywhere.

Then I knew that Molly was using the cane. In a bare spot they had stopped to rest and probably eat. There was the letter "M" scratched in the bare soil with a few leaves kicked over it. I was elated at this find because I just knew Molly was using the cane and really believed that I might be following to rescue her.

I had to follow much more slowly from there on, while hoping that I wouldn't loose the trail. Molly and her captors were traveling faster and better, more traveled paths and on much more level ground. I had to avoid the trail as it seemed to be well used, and I could meet up with a warrior at any time. I stayed in the deep woods but checked the trail every day. I still found the marks of Molly's cane, and I marveled at her act of needing it and yet seeming to be able to keep up. If she had slowed her captors up too much, they would have killed her.

After several days I came to an Indian village. Whether Molly was here or had been taken to some other village I had no idea. I camped far from the village, changing sleeping places every night. I checked on the trails beyond the village, looking for Molly's cane marks, but I found none. This didn't mean much, for the squaws were very cruel to prisoners and would have taken it away from her for no other reason than that she wanted to use it. They would make a slave out of her.

I spied on the village as much as possible from a distance, staying upwind so the dogs wouldn't scent me. The squaws would probably cut off her long blond hair and dress her like a squaw, making it difficult to recognize her from a long distance.

After a few days I could see two squaws seeming to boss another squaw or slave while she worked. I remembered that Ed had told me that most tribes had as slaves white women or captured squaws from enemy tribes. If this was a slave, her head was wrapped up in some Indian garb so her blond hair wouldn't help. Most likely it had been cut short.

After I had been watching the village for about

two weeks, the braves left the village. When the men didn't return that night, I decided they had gone for a hunting trip, or even a raid. In the morning I ventured closer as the braves were not likely to return until later in the day. As I was watching, out of the tepee came the slave and the two squaw guards. Suddenly the slave removed the garb from her head. Blond hair fell nearly to her waist. Molly! This was Molly! She held both arms above her head as she slowly turned around and around, just like she was performing a ceremonial dance. The two squaws stood perfectly still. Then Molly tied the garb back around her head, covering her hair. Then she started working, following the squaw's instructions.

I lay like I was frozen.

How in the world had Molly been able to keep her blond hair? How had she been able to cause her captors to allow this? I thought to myself, "If these Indians are as smart as they think they are, they will send her back home or kill her before she takes over the tribe."

The braves returned. I stayed much farther from the camp now that I knew that Molly was there. I couldn't take unnecessary chances of being discovered.

Autumn came. Again most of the braves left, probably to hunt for the meat supply for winter. Again I ventured closer and watched Molly's ritual of letting her hair down, while she stretched her arms and head skyward to the sun and then turned slowly around and around. By now many other Indians were coming to watch, standing perfectly still, almost in awe. Then she would put her hair under the garb and go to work under the direction of the two squaws.

Now they had her gathering the crops in the fields. Many squaws were also gathering crops, but Molly and her squaws always seemed to work some distance from the other workers.

By this time I reasoned that Molly had convinced the tribe that there was magic in the blond hair, and they dared not make the gods angry. More than likely it was the sun as she seemed to perform this ritual while lifting her head and arms toward the sun. Had Molly been able to learn sign language in such a short time? I could only believe that she had.

Now I had to find a way to let her know that I was near. I knew she had found ways to leave signs for someone who might be trying to rescue her, but I didn't believe I was as smart as Molly. It finally occurred to me that Molly was working an area of the fields to herself except for her guards. That night I slipped into that area of the field and left two ordinary sticks in the shape of a T. I had to do this only once. As I watched from a distance, when Molly came to work after her morning sun ritual, she stopped where the sticks were and looked toward the hill where she thought I was probably watching. She slowing picked up both sticks, one in each hand, looked again toward the hill, and casually tossed them away. It was clear she understood.

That night I left sticks again in the shape of an arrow pointing to the hill where she had looked the day before. Once again Molly made it clear that she understood. She looked in my direction. Her guards didn't seem to notice.

The next morning there was a change in her ritual. Instead of holding her arms up toward the sun and turning, she raised only one of her arms. Too late I realized that I hadn't starting counting at first. Surely the number of times she raised her arms had some meaning. The next day I counted more carefully. It was ten times, but one time one arm did not go all the way up. Did this mean nineteen? I thought that it did. The next day her arms went up nine times. The following day her arms went up nine times except for once when one arm went only half way up. She was definitely giving a count. It had to be for the day she would escape. She was making one other change in her ritual. Each time she finished pointing her arms toward the sun she would slowly bring her arms down, pointing toward the west. Surely she meant to leave near sunset.

There were still a lot of problems. How did Molly know that the braves would not be back when we were ready to run? There was no way to outrun them. There was the problem of moonlight at night. I could figure this out. The moon would be about one quarter full and perfect for us, just enough light to see our path but not enough to be seen at a distance if there was no cloud cover or rain. If there was rain we would leave tracks and could be followed. Had Molly thought of all this, and how would she know that the braves would not be in camp? The braves would surely have returned long before this. Yet, by this time I had almost utter faith in Molly's reasoning, so I began making plans, just believing that she knew. The Indians would surely begin to realize that she was doing a count with her morning sun ritual. I had to make my plans based on my belief in this most exceptional girl.

First, there was food. I had had no problem during the summer. I had been eating berries and roots and occasionally killed game, but only when I was far away from the village where I could dig a hole and build a small fire to cook the game. I also got fresh vegetables from the Indian fields. We couldn't do this while on the run. The corn began to ripen in the fields, so I began to steal some and place it into packets which I made from animal skins.

By this time I knew where their canoes were kept, several miles away, and in two or three different creeks which were large enough to float a canoe.

What would we do if it was pitch dark or rain-ing? I gathered pine knots and hid them along more than one trail. These would only help our pursuers if the braves or warriors were in camp. I had to plan that Molly knew that they would be gone. That meant that if it was real dark or rainy we would use the torches and simply have to outrun the squaws, the old men and the young boys left in the village.

Then the braves returned. Molly kept up her sun ritual every day the sun shone, giving her countdown. The tribe stood stock still and watched almost in awe.

About three days later the braves began a war dance. They were going on a raiding party to the settlements, probably to the nearest one in Kentucky. I had to adjust my plans to avoid that direction, but I still had no idea how Molly knew this. Almost all of the grown warriors left with their bodies covered with war paint. Five days were left before we were to try to escape.

I was relieved to see Molly and her guards come back to the fields. I hadn't been able to get close to the village but pretty well knew that Molly and the squaws had been drying the meat the hunters had brought in. This was good. The workers would be busy with harvesting in the fields until after our escape date.

Molly's ritual showed four days left. That night, I left three sticks for Molly so that when she saw them the next morning, she'd know we were on the same count. On the final date her arms only went over her head; then her arms pointed west.

Molly was in the fields all day with her squaws near her. Would she be worn out by sunset? All day long she seemed to be sick, often holding her stomach, often going to the edge of the field in order not to pollute the crops. Her guards didn't seem to be much concerned. She had been doing this for a few days. After all, where could she go without being caught was probably the way they would see it.

Just as the sun was about to set, holding her stomach, she came to the edge of the field and then started running straight toward me. I had been worried about her really being sick, but she had been saving energy, as well as fooling the squaws into giving her a running start. It worked perfectly. The fat squaws started running after her. Molly slowed down. The squaws kept running as they were gaining ground. I was worried that she was really sick. After she got them out of hearing distance of the other workers, she began running free and easy. Her guards stopped and howled for help. It was a few minutes before they had to go back so they could be heard.

Suddenly I was in her path with the food pack over my shoulders and ready to go. We gave each other one quick embrace and were on our way, never saying a word.

Now I was in charge of the escape plans. I felt inadequate after watching this girl for several months. The night was perfect. Just enough moonlight to see our trail and not enough to be seen easily. I was beginning to believe, as the Indians apparently did, that she had power over the sun.

We followed the trail to a small stream, waded down the stream for a mile or so and stepped on a large flat rock and carefully stepped on other rocks for some distance. We then had to travel through rugged woodland until we were on another trail that I had scouted. This we followed to a large creek where we found several canoes. I had also hidden one in case the warriors had taken them.

We walked through much of the night before we stopped again to sleep. There was a dim moonlight to show our way. She slept in my arms. This was the first time my arms had been around her and it left me feeling that she had always belonged there. When we woke about nine, I told Molly that it was safe to talk if we liked. We were now located between two regular Indian trails and far from either of them.

Again we traveled until near daylight and hid during the day. I had scouted this area during the summer and knew we had about one day's travel left before we would run into the warriors' path. From Ed I knew about where the warriors' trails were. One was up the Great Kanawha where Mary Ingles and the Dutch woman had traveled a few years before after escaping from the Indians. The second one crossed at the mouth of the Sandy River. We had come that way. The third one led to the Kentucky settlements where Daniel Boone and a man named Harrod had built forts. According to Ed, these were about one hundred miles below the mouth of the Sandy River. We had to avoid these paths.

The next night we hid the canoe about midnight and headed south walking. I was hoping to come to the Ohio about midway between Sandy and Limestone rivers. I think we came to the Ohio pretty close to where I hoped. I spent one day looking for Indian signs and hoped to find a hidden canoe. I found neither but found a part of a tree trunk big enough to float both of us. We paddled and swam to cross the Ohio, landing about a mile downstream.

We walked inland for two days and camped where we found a lot of nuts, wild grapes and other fruits. We decided to stay and gather food. I had seen no sign of Indians nor even buffalo trails.

By now we felt safe to talk and discuss plans of where and how to go. After watching Molly all summer, I held her ability to think almost unbeatable. After all, she had thought one step ahead of a whole Indian village.

We began to gather food for the long winter in case we decided to stay here. In the last two weeks of her captivity Molly had learned to dry meat or to mix meat with certain herbs, nuts and fruit. I hunted every day. Game was plentiful.

I discussed with Molly about whether we should

go west to the Kentucky settlement or go home, which was a much longer and harder journey. We could stay where we were until spring and start. We couldn't carry enough food to sustain us, but by spring we could get more food from the land. The Indians wouldn't be out as much in the winter, but travel might be impossible. The Indians were still on the warpath, so we decided to stay.

I had to find shelter. Earlier I had seen a large hollow sycamore tree. When I went back to it again it seemed to be big enough to suit our needs, so we moved into our new home.

Every evening we talked about her capture and how she survived. It was a fascinating story! She gave me most of the credit because I had told her the stories Ed had told me. The key was the stories about Indian superstitions. After her capture the Indians traveled fast and long hours. They didn't annoy her much as long as she kept up and did most of the camp work plus cooking. They slapped her around a little while showing her how they wanted her to cook. She learned a few of their signs and a few words.

The leader of the group was high tempered. The others used a word when they glanced at him from a distance which she thought to be "angry." They also seemed to be fascinated by her blond hair. She thought she could use this as a superstition, so that was when she started a little ritual of raising her arms to the sun and holding up her hair, hoping to discourage them from scalping her for the blond scalp. Every time a brave touched her hair she would react by pointing at the hair and then at the sun, and using the word she believed to mean "angry." They would just shout and laugh.

When the party finally slowed down a little, feeling they were beyond danger from a rescue party, they began to treat her a little rougher. One day one of the braves grabbed a lock of hair and cut it off. Molly said she put on a show, pointing at her hair and the sun, and again saying the word she thought they used to mean angry. She also pointed at him and made motions meaning death.

She had planned for this type of incident.

She was allowed to get herbs to use in cooking. She had gathered leaves from a plant that would cause illness when eaten. As she served the man who cut the lock of hair she managed to get some of these dried powdered leaves into his food, which was in a bowl made of bark. He got deathly sick that night. The next day Molly pointed at her hair and the sun as the cause. From that time on they almost feared her and would never touch her hair.

They started calling her a name which later she learned meant something like "sun goddess." In the Indian village where she was taken one of the squaws guarding her knew a few words of English from having guarded other prisoners. Molly learned a lot of Indian words and was able to communicate fairly well.

I asked her how they had failed to know that she was signaling numbers to me. She said that almost at the same time she knew the Indians began to worry about too much rain before their crops were gathered. They were calling on the rain gods. Her guard was able to communicate this to her. Molly indicated to them that she could ask for twenty days of sunshine, but no more, for the sun god would be angry. She showed how she would ask. Each day she could only ask for one day less. She could only hope that Indian summer would last that long. She knew that twenty days would pass before the moon would be right.

She would often repeat, "I knew Tom would be the only one who could save me." I loved to have her tell me this over and over. She said she thought about everyone in the settlement and rejected them one by one because of family responsibilities or lack of experience in the woods. She analyzed Jake, her boyfriend. She concluded that he was only tough sounding without basic strength. My friend, Ed, was long past his prime and crippled. I was the only one left, the boy who was called "Useless Tom." She thought of me the same way, as just a young boy who wouldn't even work around the farm.

She said, "I thought to myself, he isn't a boy anymore. He's really strong and very tall and big boned. Has he grown up mentally tough? I thought of all the things he had told me about the woods. I was seeing that what he told me was true about the trees and the plants. Even the lay of the land was as he told me. The nature of the Indians he learned from Ed is right. Is he brave enough, mature enough, and does he love me enough?" She said, "I had to remember how you looked at me and loved to talk with me. Maybe it was because I was the only one who liked to listen to you. I finally believed that there was more to it than that. By then I knew that you would follow me."

We discussed our future. We would go back home to see her folks and see our neighbors and thank Ed whose knowledge had save Molly's life. Molly said, "I can't wait to show you off—"Useless Tom"—now big and strong enough to whip a bear. Useless Tom who went into the middle of wild Indian country and brought me home. I can't wait to tell them and to brag on my Tom."

By then we both knew that we would always be together. We could be man and wife today or any time. The preacher could marry us when we saw one. This was a regular practice on the frontier. We didn't have a broom we could step over.

We talked this over and decided to be cool and practical. If Molly became pregnant at once, we wouldn't be leaving for several months. How could a pregnant woman make that journey? But then, how could they travel with a small baby later?

That very night it turned really cold. We did not have enough furs tanned yet to keep us warm.

Molly brought her covers and crept close beside me. Later we talked. She said she couldn't believe how big and strong I had gotten in my chest and shoulders. She raised my deerskin and rubbed my chest as she talked. I lifted her deerskin and held her close to me. Our noble plans of a few hours before just melted.

After all, couldn't two people who had outsmarted a whole tribe of Indians find the way home?

As we lay in each other's arms we agreed that we would always love the bitter cold that drove us to sharing each other, thus making the months of fear and hardship worthwhile.

A little later Molly asked to run her hand over my chest. She was almost talking to herself, saying, "My Tom, so strong, with the strength of a bear. With strength so much deeper than broad shoulders and strong muscles."

I knew that together we could meet any challenge that life might hold for us.

THE RESCUE-PART TWO
Molly's Story

My family, the Prestons, had moved to western Virginia to buy land and farm three years before. My father built a log cabin and cleared land for farming. This was Indian country, a dangerous place to live but an opportunity to prosper. In the time that we were there we had several Indian raids and scares. Other settlers were living in the area but not closer to each other. Often Indians would attack a family, burn the cabin and kill and scalp the family or sometimes capture a family member to keep as a slave.

Sometimes Indians were seen and the families made their way to a fort, fighting the Indians until everyone could return to their farms when the raiders left.

My family had been attacked a couple of times by small Indian bands and we were able to fight them off successfully.

I was now sixteen years old which was almost an old maid on the frontier. Everyone said that I was pretty with very light blond hair and deep violet-blue eyes. I had several offers for marriage but hadn't decided whether I yet wanted to be married. It was understood that I might marry Jake Clay, a nineteen-year-old neighbor boy. I supposed that I would marry Jake who was a big burly boy and who was a little bit of a bully. He sometimes talked a little loud and tough but when he outgrew it I would probably marry Jake. Other boys stopped by to see me also.

One boy who came by sometimes to talk was a

young boy, Tom Wilson. Tom was just a little younger then me, although I thought of him as much younger. He had always been much smaller then me. I thought of him as a younger brother not as a boyfriend. In the last year he had grown almost a foot and was tall and gawky looking.

A lot of people called him 'Useless Tom." He could not be kept around the family farm working but was always in the woods hunting or visiting with an old crippled-up Indian fighter. His family just quit trying to get Tom to work on the farm and let him bring wild game for the table. He often stopped at our cabin leaving wild game for our table.

When he stopped by he would talk to me a lot even though he was shy with most people. We talked a lot about the plants of the woods, Indians, and woodlands. Plants and the bark of trees was my special interest. I had learned so much about them from my grandmother, a herb doctor. I wanted to follow her footsteps as there were no trained doctors anywhere that I knew about.

Tom talked a lot about Indians and their ways, strange to our settlers. He had learned so much from an old frontiersman, Ed Luther, who he visited often.

Sometimes we talked about Mary Ingles and other white women who had been made captives by Indians. All of them were either killed or made slaves, sometimes being used by the braves as play objects. Ed Luther had told him that almost all prisoners who survived had figured out a way to take advantage of the Indians' belief in omens and superstitions. When Tom told me this, I gave little thought to it, not knowing that later my very survival would depend on this knowledge of Indian superstition. At that time it didn't seem serious, nor did Tom for that matter. I just seemed to think of him as "Useless Tom," just taking other people's opinion-not my own.

Then one day I was an Indian captive, just that sudden. Late one evening I went for the cows to drive them home to milk. I wandered off the path to find some early spring plants for medicine. Suddenly I was grabbed from behind around the neck. When the arm was released a knife was held at my throat until my arms were tied and I was gagged. Three Indians were in the group. They motioned for me to walk ahead of them. At night I was tied to a tree.

The second day we walked until we met with the entire raiding party of about thirty-six braves. Some of them showed a lot things stolen during their raid, including several fresh scalps. I thought I could recognize a couple of them as scalps of neighbors.

When we got farther along the trail my arms were untied and I was made to carry a heavy load as I walked. I put on my first act at that time by pretending to stagger and fall behind with the load. My load was lightened some and I could carry it easily. I was much stronger than I looked but I wanted to keep my strength in case I had a chance to escape.

The Indians split into three parties of about a dozen in each party. This was to confuse the settlers who would be following them so that they wouldn't know which party I might be with. It was important that I leave some sign to guide the rescuers if they followed. I would have to think of something. I didn't know what. At first I had an idea. I was made to walk near the front with a lead scout ahead of me, his eyes always watching ahead for danger.

The first day the braves I was with stopped to eat at noon. By motions and signs I was able to show that I needed some strips of cloth, which they had stolen to tie the pack I was carrying around my shoulders. They watched as I cut strips of cloth and tied them to the packs and secured them around my shoulder. They didn't notice that the ends of the strips were a little longer then needed as I tied them into bows. As we walked that afternoon I was able to tear little ends from the strips and put them in my dress pocket. A couple of times that afternoon I stumbled and fell on purpose as I climbed up a steep bank. Each time I was able to leave a little piece of cloth hidden under the leaves.

As I walked and at night I thought a lot about who might rescue me. I knew that a lot of settlers would start on the trail and probably be led by a man named Hawk Hayes. I knew they would follow until we got to Indian country. They would have to turn back as it would be too dangerous. Even if the settlers caught up with the warriors who had me, they would probably kill me at the first sign of attack. Would there be anyone who might follow to rescue me, maybe Jake, the man who expected to marry me? For the first time I really gave thought to his character and how he would react to danger. I concluded that Jake Clay was better at talk than deed. He would never face this danger. Most of the men were married and had families to protect at home.

At last I gave thought to Tom, the boy everyone called "Useless Tom," who had talked to me a lot about Indians. I suddenly began to realize that Tom was no longer a boy but was almost overnight becoming a man. Not only growing taller but filling out. He would soon be a big man. Everything that I had heard about Indian ways I was now trying to recall. Most of what I now needed to know and was remembering had been told to me by Tom: the things he had learned from Ed Luther.

Would Tom, who I had often thought of as a boy, care enough to follow me? I thought a lot about our relations with each other. I had always listened to him and did like to hear his stories. We had a common interest in trees and plants, I recalled that he always flashed a big smile when he met me and talked a lot to me, though he was reserved with everyone else. I remembered how he sometimes looked at me, then I knew he was in love with me and I had never even taken him seriously. After thinking about this I concluded that Tom would follow. This gave me hope. I would help leave some trail when possible, but first I needed to survive. I began to plan how to take advantage of the Indians' superstitious nature.

I already had a clue on something which might be used. My captors seemed to be curious about my blond hair. I must have been the first real light blond they ever saw. They would often point at my hair and talk among themselves.

Within a couple of days on the trail, more burdens were placed on me. I now was made to build the campfire at the end of the day and make stew from small game killed during the day. As the pot boiled I would look for plants and roots growing nearby to add to the stew. I was able to make signs to explain what I wanted to do with these plants. They watched me carefully as I gathered and cleaned them, then made me eat a few to show that they weren't poisonous. They seemed to like the stew with the additions and even allowed me to gather a few when we stopped for a noon hour break. I was tied up every night to a tree or sapling. Sometimes I was able to make the letter "M" in the soil then cover it with leaves. Every morning I had to cover the hole dug out for our camp fire then cover the loose soil with leaves. Sometimes I was able to make an "M" in the loose soil.

After a few days they no longer seemed concerned with pursuit and traveled more slowly, even stopping to hunt or catch fish or maybe to scout for enemies. The slower pace caused more problems for me. I was treated more roughly. I had already used my blond hair to make them wonder a little. Every day when we stopped or stayed for awhile in camp I made a show of shaking my long blond hair out while looking at the sun and talking or chanting a poem I knew.

They seemed a little awed about my performance but had said nothing. I knew by now that the leader had some problems with one of the braves and maybe a challenge for leadership. The brave used me to show off to the other braves by bullying me around a little and I guessed by making lewd remarks about me. Some of the other braves would laugh. The leader would not let him go too far. I might be valuable property for trade with my people.

One morning before we started on our way, was shaking out my hair and going through my ritual. The bully brave decided to show off. He came to me and whacked off a lock of my hair. By now I felt that I was safe from much harm until they knew whether someone would ransom me. As soon as the bully cut off the lock of my hair I went into a little tantrum. I pointed at the sun, then at the bully, shook my fist and kept repeating a word I learned from them meaning, "angry, angry." The bully looked a little shocked. I wasn't through with him yet. I was ready. I had found a plant several days before and kept grinding it up into powder. By now I was in the habit of serving the stew in plates made of bark. I served the bully pretending to be mad at him. On his stew was some of the powder. He was a sick Indian before the night was over. The leader wouldn't let the bully bother me, but seemed pleased. The next morning I talked to the sun, pointed to my missing lock of hair, then pointed to the bully, who looked scared. On the rest of the journey no one seemed willing to risk the wrath of the sun.

They even let me begin to wash my hair when we were waiting for the scouts or hunters on the trail. When they seemed impatient with something as silly as washing my hair, I would point at the sun and repeat their word meaning "angry."

It was important that I needed to keep my blond hair washed. If Tom was following he could recognize me from a long distance. We arrived at the Indian village deep in the Ohio country, I supposed. We had crossed the Ohio River in canoes the Indians had hidden on their way to our settlement.

As soon as we entered camp, I was turned over to the squaws. My captors seemed glad to be rid of me as they seemed to fear me and my protection from the sun. I was made a slave by the squaws. Two older squaws were now my mistresses. They had heard from my captors about my blond hair and strange powers through it with the sun.

The squaws were mean and bossy. They didn't believe my captors or didn't share their superstitions. They would show me by making me run the gauntlet. I was stripped to the waist and made to run through two lines of women and children holding switches with thorns, sticks and clubs. Before I was given the signal to start, I held up my arms while looking at the sun with my long hair in my hands.

Then I was hit in the back, my signal to run. I was hit with everything as I ran. My back was bleeding from thorns, switches, and sticks. I staggered, fell and ran some more. Toward the end of the line were heavier clubs. I was hit in the shoulder with one of them causing me to stagger to one side almost falling. One of the squaws grabbed me by the hair, pulling me toward her. This caused another one from the other side to miss me with her club and hit the squaw who had grabbed my hair on the back of the head. I staggered the few feet to the end of the line in a bloody looking condition and hurting. The squaw who had grabbed my hair was unconscious and nearly died. This left the other squaws in some awe and fear of my hair as they hadn't seen the hair-grabber hit in the head.

At least they were left with enough doubt that when I recovered I was allowed to wash my hair and go through my ritual to the sun. The two squaws, who I was assigned to as a slave, were now a little afraid of me but not so much that they didn't make me work hard. They often hit me or poked me with a sharp stick.

The worst of the two squaws was named Minko which meant skunk cabbage. I thought she was well named except that I didn't see any reason for the cabbage in her name. Minko had been in charge of other white prisoners before me and had learned a lot of English words. This gave me an idea for learning more Indian language. When Minko gave me orders I would act confused and dumb until she repeated the orders in broken English, accompanying the words with a blow from a stick. One of the ways I got a little bit even was to smile and say, "Thank you, mother of mongrels." Minko knew the English word "dog" but had never heard "mongrel." When she asked what it meant, I would tell her "angel." She became proud of her new name.

I was going to make them a little more superstitious about my protection from the sun. I had been making plans all along since I found that bothering my hair left them scared. Just before my capture one of the visitors to our home had an almanac, which gave a date for an eclipse of the sun. I remembered the date and started counting the days. To be sure I was counting right I picked up ten small pebbles and placed them in one of the pockets of my dress, Every morning I put a pebble in the other pocket then counted ten more days moving a pebble back every day. If I had counted right the eclipse would be in twelve more days. Then I started putting on an act.

Every morning in my ritual and chant I raised an arm twelve times, the next morning eleven, counting down to one. When Minko got impatient with my "foolish" hair washing and rituals every day I would point at the sun and say the Indian word for "angry." When I started the counting of days I would hold up fingers showing the days left. This had no meaning to her and she would hit me with her stick.

When the day the eclipse was due, I had Minko so angry by taking extra time washing my hair that I wasn't allowed time to wash it, which I had hoped would happen. She was extra cruel to me that morning, driving me to do my work and hitting me with a stick. I kept her mad by pointing at the sun often and saying 'angry."

Then the eclipse started. Of course they had seen eclipses before, but I could soon see that the entire village was scared. Everyone was watching me and began blaming Minko for causing the trouble by mistreating me. I knew this to be almost a total eclipse. I started chanting and performing my ritual while warming my hair with my hands. When I believed that it was time for the eclipse to be over and start receding, I was ready. I began to make signs pointing to my hair then at the creek water. When I ran toward the water and started washing my hair, the tribe, including the, braves watched. Then I began my sun ritual, chanting and warming my fresh washed, sun-colored blond hair. The eclipse continued to recede. I continued my ritual and chants until the eclipse was over. In the chants I kept apologizing for the "Mother of Mongrels." Only Minko could understand this. It left her scared but angry, angry enough to start giving me work orders, and raising her stick on me. This caused the tribe to make her stop with warnings of disaster. They were impressed and scared, as I wanted them to be, especially the braves.

The braves were my biggest worry. The stories of their treatment of white slave girls was always on my mind. I had them scared of the "Sun Goddess" as I was now sometimes called. I was pleased with my performance during the eclipse and felt I wouldn't be harmed much while they believed the sun might cause them harm.

I knew that Minko would be more angry than ever and not as scared as the others. Even though Minko would try to get revenge, she wouldn't dare go too far, as the tribe would stop her.

Then another problem arose: a medicine man came. He was an immediate danger. He was jealous of the powers the tribe believed I had. He and Minko started plotting to prove me a fake. The medicine man was trying to prove that I had no special power through my hair. Minko tried to aid him any way she could. I had to keep the tribe scared and superstitious, and thought desperately for an idea.

Then, I had a clue. I noticed that the medicine man broke out with a skin rash, and found that it was from poison vines. Maybe poison oak or poison ivy. I hoped that it was one of these, because neither of them bothered me. This gave me a good idea. I added a new act to my morning ritual. I began to place a cloth with the design of the sun on it in my apron pocket. I would reach into my pocket and rub the damp cloth as I went through my ritual. I tried to make it look as if I was acting secretive, but made sure Minko saw this.

Then one morning the sun cloth was missing, as I suspected it would be. I went ahead through my ritual without it. The crowd was there as usual. Before they could leave, the medicine man appeared waving my sun cloth in the air. He made a speech to tell how he had recurred the cloth to test its powers, and found it powerless. To further show how powerless it was he rubbed it all over his body face and hands. What he didn't know was that the dampness in the cloth came from poisonous plant and vines. The next morning he was swelled up horribly, and left totally disgraced. The tribe feared my powers even more. I began to plan an escape, in case Tom had failed to follow. I still believed he was somewhere near the camp, but had no way of knowing for sure.

I began to plan an escape in case Tom had failed to follow. I still believed that he was somewhere near the camp, but had no way of knowing for sure. I planned to escape in either case. Going alone was almost impossible, but I planned to try if there was no sign from Tom.

I thought and tried to remember everything I had heard about the geography of the country. I knew that Mary Ingles and the Dutch woman had escaped from miles below on the Ohio River. They had followed up the Ohio River to the Kanawha and New Rivers into Virginia near to where I had been captured. I was sure that I had been brought down the Big Sandy River to the Ohio River.

I wasn't sure whether I would recognize either river when I saw it. I knew the general direction we had traveled after my capture was northwest, so my home lay southeast. I had one advantage over Mary Ingles. I was sure that I knew edible plants and roots better.

I gave consideration to escaping in the fall or spring. The time when there would be more food to sustain me. It would also be when the braves in the tribe would be making raids or hunting, leaving only young boys and old men to follow my trail. I learned more and more of the Indian language and began to know their plans. They didn't know how much of their language I understood. Maybe they wouldn't even care as the idea of a girl escaping from the middle of

Indian settlements was almost unbelievable.

Then I was sent to the fields to work for the first time. Minko and the other squaw were always with me. I was still allowed to wash my hair every morning and perform my sun ritual. Minko didn't dare stop this as the tribe was still sure stopping this would lead to disaster. As soon as the ritual was over they made me tie my hair up with a scarf and go to the fields to work. I soon found that Minko insisted that the three of us work apart from the other squaws. This gave her a chance to hit me sometimes and not be seen. This suited my plans so I kept Minko a little angry most of the time.

As we cultivated the crops, I was always kept between them working. I was kept in front of them working. Maybe to be where they could watch me or perhaps where Minko could give me a whack. One morning we started to work on the three rows where we had stopped the night before. As I started to work on my row, I saw two sticks lying where I had stopped working the evening before. The sticks were lying forming the letter "T." I was so surprised that it was several seconds before I thought to kick them aside. Was this an accident or had Tom placed them there? I believed that it was Tom. If it was Tom more signs would follow. That evening I started piling weeds beside my row just before we quit. Would my guards notice and be suspicious in the change in my work habits? Every morning I would remove the weeds, looking for any sign from Tom. I wasn't disappointed. The very next morning, he left sticks in the shape of an arrow pointing toward a small hill. Then I knew where he was hiding. My guards seemed not to notice.

A few days later underneath the weeds, the letter "T' was marked into the soil. It was hard to keep from screaming in joy as I walked through the "T" rubbing it out. That evening I managed to mark an "M" in the soil before piling some weeds over it. The next morning the "M" was gone. Tom would now know that I had received his message.

I didn't get any more signs from Tom for awhile. I understood why. The braves had been gone for awhile. Probably on spring raids on the Kentucky or Virginia settlements. Most of them were back now and Tom would stay away until they left again. It would be autumn before they left in large numbers, first to hunt for a supply of meat for the winter and maybe later to go on raids. I often overheard their plans as they had no idea how much of their language I now understood.

I continued to raise and lower my arms counting days. I felt that before long this would be useful when I wanted to signal Tom.

I was getting pretty good at Indian sign language. I made explanations for my countdown by sign language. One excuse was that rain was needed for the crops. They believed that I was beseeching the sun to bring rain. The rains came three days before the end of my countdown. Since the rains continued for about a week, the tribe seemed to believe that, I brought the rains even if the countdown wasn't exact.

Then I began a countdown for the longest day of the year as I kept an exact count for the month and date. By this time I understood how the Indian calendar worked, the thirteen moons in a year. I knew in advance by counting the exact date that each full moon would fall by the white man's calendar. This gave me a double check on the date in case Minko should see me using my counting pebbles and throw them away.

I found other reasons for countdowns, such as the next full moon or harvest moon, and sometimes no countdowns at all. Many of the braves left for awhile to go to a big council meeting. I received another "T" sign from Tom in the field where I always left a pile of weeds. I knew that this was to reassure me that he was watching once in a awhile.

When most of the braves left to hunt for game to dry for the winter food supply, more signs were left by Tom. The usual 'T." I replied with "M." Tom had the message. No more messages were exchanged for awhile. The braves returned from the hunt. It would be dangerous for Tom to stay close to camp with the braves in the woods around camp. Besides, Tom couldn't read my signs except when there was some moonlight.

I overheard enough talk to know that a big raid was planned at the next full moon. It was to be a big one into the settlements. Braves from many villages were to join together. Preparations were made, guns were cleaned, tomahawks, arrows and lances were sharpened. War dances were held; wild, scary affairs. I only peeped out of my wigwam. In the excitement I might not be safe. They might lose their fear of the "Sun Goddess."

I felt safe in the mornings when the warriors were exhausted from the war dance of the night before. I continued my morning ritual and started another countdown. The war party was to start in fifteen days, so I started at twenty. If Tom was watching from far away I just hoped he would guess what this count meant. This count gave us five days after the warriors left so that they would be far away.

Tom wouldn't get too close to the camp while all the braves were there, but I was sure that he would watch from some hill some distance away until I performed my morning ritual, and guess why I was counting as soon as most of the warriors left on their raid.

My work was still in the fields and by this time we were gathering crops. I kept Minko irritated so that she managed to keep me away from the other workers who were a little scared to have me mistreated. The rest of the warriors finally left the next morning.

The next morning in my ritual I gave my count of three. In the field I found three sticks. Tom and I were on the same count. What time should I run? I decided late in the afternoon since I had no signal from Tom. That morning I raised my left hand we first met on my escape when I had told him, "I knew that you would be the one who would find me."

We started walking just before dark again. Tom led the way, carrying his rifle and pack of food and supplies. Tom refused to let me carry anything until I was used to running and walking again. As I followed him I marveled at the change in him in such a short time. From a gangly boy, he was bigger in the shoulders and chest, and strong looking. He acted confident and seemed to have plans worked out for our exact escape route.

We walked through much of the night before we stopped again to sleep. There was a dim moonlight to show our way. I slept in Tom's arms. This was the first time his arms had ever been around me, but left me feeling that I had always belonged there. When we woke about nine, Tom told me that we were safe to talk if we liked. He said that we were now between two regular Indian trails and far from either of them. There was little danger from the Indian camp where I had been a prisoner since all of the braves from that camp were on their raid. Only older men, young boys, and squaws had been left to follow our tail. The danger the first two days had been Indian braves from other villages who hadn't gone on raids but might be hunting or lurking in the woods.

Tom explained his plan of escape. We were to avoid the main trails between the warriors going to Limestone Creek in central Kentucky and the one up the Big Sandy River, the one I had traveled as a captive. He said that we would travel between these two warriors' paths to avoid raiding parties. This would take us far out of our way.

We made our way to the Ohio River and crossed on a dead log, floating and using a long pole pushing the log across the river. We made our way deeper into Kentucky and found a big hollow tree for a temporary home until the country would be free of raiding Indian parties. The trails would not be safe until winter weather. We might not get home until spring. I wanted to see my people and neighbors but loved my shelter in a hollow sycamore tree, with Tom.

We talked a lot about our future together and made plans. We could be man and wife at any time, then be married formally when a minister made his way to our settlement. This was the practice on the frontier. We made plans to wait until we were back home. If we were delayed until spring it could be a rough trip for a pregnant girl. We decided to lay apart at night. We needed to be practical. But that night the winds rose and whistled around us. It got cold, waking me. I snuggled closer to Tom, trying to get warm. He put his arms around me and under my buckskin jacket. We both just forgot to be practical any longer. When we finally made our way home we would belong to each other as man and wife.

Now I wanted to get home and show off my man to the neighbors. The boy they had called "Useless Tom" was now returning as a man who had gone on a mission where none of them would have dared to go, to rescue me. I would make him a famous frontiersman.

Tom guessed that we were two hundred miles from home when we started. It took us almost two weeks to travel home. We had to avoid the easier trails along the streams and paths made by animals. This is where the Indians might have seen our tracks. Instead we followed a long ridge traversing up and down over the mountains. The weather was good. Tom had become an excellent woodsman, and obtained our food from natures bounty. We jokingly referred to these two weeks as our honeymoon. By the middle of the second week the landscapes became more familiar, and I knew we were nearing home.

We spent one last honeymoon night together, and left early before the fog had completely lifted that morning. By mid-morning we cleared a knob hill, and saw the first open field. It was the fields at home, my home. We topped another hill, I could see our barn. From the direction we were approaching it obstructed my view of the house. I was nervous; was the family all right? I began to hear the familiar sounds of farm life, but could see no one or hear no human voice. It was now afternoon and everyone could be anywhere on the farm, busy with the days chores.

We were no less than one hundred feet from the barn. Suddenly, the farm door swung open. It was my sister, Mary, carrying a bucket of feed, for the chickens. As she turned and saw us she let out a startled cry. Who could these scraggly looking strangers be? She stopped totally frozen for a moment. Then raced towards us screaming. "Molly! Molly!" She hugged me so hard she tackled me. "Molly, you are real, you're not a ghost, you're alive! Thank you, stranger, for bringing back my sister," she said. "Thank you."

Laughing Tom offered us both a hand and lifted us from the ground. "Stranger, huh? Mary that's no way to talk about someone you've known you entire life." She looked up. "Oh my God, Tom Wilson." We were all laughing now.

Then my little brother, Joe, came running around the barn to see what all the commotion was about. As he turned the corner he slipped and fell, his jaw dropped in disbelief. Little Joe, your gonna' draw flies with your mouth open like that.

Don't you have anything to say to your oldest sister, Molly? Joe scrambled to his feet and ran back the way he came, screaming, "Molly's home! Molly's home!" Tom left us to see his family a few farms away, while Mary and I headed for the house. We barely rounded the barn when we met Mom and the two younger children. Mom could barely speak for her tears, but she could hug like a bear and I thought she would never turn me loose. "I thought we'd lost you forever." She sobbed. From the hills I could hear the echoes "Molly's home, Molly Preston's home!" The call relayed across the settlement, shouted from hill to hill, and finally to the valley. First my family came in from the fields. Then the near neighbors came, and folks from town. Everyone hugged me and cried, asking questions at the same time. In spite of my younger brothers and sisters hugging my legs, everyone wanted to hear my story. I would begin to tell it, then more people would arrive and the process would start again. I barely got a chance to tell anybody anything.

Finally, my father climbed on top of the table and called for quiet. His eyes were red, his cheeks still wet with tears. "My Molly has been home, but for three hours she hasn't eaten, she hasn't got a chance to wash up. I thank you all for being here, but if Molly has a story to tell, she'll tell it when she's good and ready. Why don't you folks go on home now." And with that the crowd began to crumble.

I tugged my fathers pant leg and he bent down from atop the table. "It's okay, Father," I whispered. "These folks have a right to know, and I do want to tell them." My father lifted me up to the table and announced to the crowd, "Molly is going to speak to you now, but only a few questions please. After what my little girl has been through, she deserves some rest."

Jake Clay, my old boyfriend asked the first

question. "When the Indians took you, that fool boy Tom Wilson followed. He hasn't been back yet. How long did he last before the braves took his scalp?" It suddenly dawned on me that Mary and I knew that Tom had rescued me and delivered me home safely. Infuriated by Jakes smug tone, I exploded, "Fool Tom? Useless Tom? Helpless Tom? I don't want to hear that ever again. Tom Wilson was the one who sneaked into the middle of that Indian camp, released me and brought me home today."

Suddenly my sister Mary jumped onto the table beside me. "I saw Tom Wilson today" she said, "I hadn't seen him in a year, but I wouldn't have known him in a hundred. He looks as big as that mountain over there. I bet he could whip a dozen braves, as well as any bear that gets in between he and Molly here.

Meanwhile at the Wilson farm, the family was busy butchering a hog. One of the boys looked down the long valley and saw someone walking. Mr. Wilson nodded, probably one of the neighbors looking to trade some corn for a bit of pork belly. Tom's twin sister, Ellen, came out of the cabin. She had kept a steady vigil for Tom for the past two weeks, just as she did during his hunting trips. She always had a hot meal waiting for his return, but he had never been gone this long before. Hearsay was that he had likely been ambushed by the same war party that had taken Molly Preston. Her father and brother had searched in vain for him but could not find nary a trace. Jake Clay had told Deacon Phillips that fool Tom is likely dead by now. If the Indians didn't get him a wild cat or bear surely did.

Ellen just knew that neither was true: Tom was her twin and he was alive, she was sure of it. Seeing the distant stranger, she let out a yell, and started out in that direction in a full sprint. Her father and brothers stopped their preparations and looked up.

Their sixteen year old sister, dress billowing behind her, looked as though she was flying. The stranger began running as well. Suddenly she leaped through the air and wrapped her arms around the strangers neck as he spun her around. "My God, Father, is it Tom?" Sam gasped. "That can't be Tom; that's one big man. Look he's swing Ellen as if she were a baby," Answered Eli. Mr. Wilson only smiled. "Ellen could always recognize Tom's walk no matter how far away he was. Boys kill a chicken for supper. We will be having a guest over for dinner tonight," Was all he said. When Ellen landed in Tom's arms tears were running down his deer skin jacket. "Everyone thought you were lost forever, but I knew you were alive. I never lost faith in you. I would have known if anything would have happened," She sobbed. "I watched for you everyday, even though everyone was saying that... that you would never be back."

After some years had passed, men who traded with the tribes came back with stories told by the Indians of the girl they had once captured, who they now called the "Sun Goddess."

According to their growing legends, the "Sun Goddess" had strange powers through the sun. She had brought rain, caused the sun to have an eclipse and could bring a curse on anyone who touched her sun-colored hair. One day this girl ran away toward the setting sun, disappearing into the forest. They had not even followed, fearing the sun curse.

In our long years together, Tom called me his "Sun Goddess" and pretended to fear what he called my "strange powers" over him.

JOHN LANE'S STORY

 I was born John Lane, the second of seven children. My parents were James and Mary Lane. We lived on a small mountain farm in southern West Virginia. The work was hard and food and clothes were scarce.

My brother Tom, who was one year older, and I went to a one-room school where, as the old song goes, "Readin, Writin, and Rithmitic was taught to the tune of a hickory stick."

We had a good country school teacher, Mr. Hays, who was strict and made sure that we learned the three R's. This was a few years after the Civil War. He often talked to us about the need to learn lest we too would end up in a mountain shack with too many kids and not enough money.

Tom and I were inspired by this but were not willing to wait for years for this to happen. We wanted to leave now and make money. Where, we had no idea. We started to inquire and study history and find out more about current events. We were lucky that we had a neighbor that we worked for sometimes from Pennsylvania. He subscribed to the *Pittsburgh Press*. He would give us the papers after he had finished with them. We learned that the mills, mines and timbermen hired boys as young as we were, even younger, to be helpers as there were no child labor laws then.

Tom and I made up our minds, we were going north, where the industries were, to get rich. It was spring and school was out. We had a few dollars saved from doing chores for the neighbors.

One warm spring morning, when Father was gone, we told Mother that we were leaving. She cried so long and hard that we almost backed out. After we showed her what we had learned about getting north and finding work, she finally gave us her blessing.

We walked to the railroad, ten miles away, to catch a ride north. A freight train rolled past. We stood and watched, scared to death at the speed it made, but we kept walking anyway.

It began to get darker and colder. We stopped beside the tracks and built a fire as we had thought to bring matches if not enough clothes. We also had brought what little food there was. It was now lonely, cold and dark. The eerie night sounds were all around us. I was scared and ready to turn back, but Tom furnished enough backbone for both of us. Suddenly we heard a voice call, "Hello the fire." One of us squeaked, "Hello." A hobo appeared, a tall thin man with clothes that were well worn but not real dirty, and asked if we had mulligan stew. We didn't even know what it was. He said he had a few vegetables and a pot. He boiled all of them in lots of water and shared the thin soup with us. We thought it was great.

We sat around the little fire and talked a long time, telling him all about us. He was horrified that we planned to hop freight trains without knowing what we were doing. He told us that even grown men trying to catch a moving train often were killed or had their legs cut off by falling under the train. He said to only hop a train when it first started out or when it slowed down going up steep grades. He gave us a lot of other advice which later was real helpful.

That night wasn't real cold for me as I slept between the hobo and Tom. I lay awake for quite awhile being homesick and lonesome. The next morning the lonesomeness and homesickness left but were replaced with hunger as nothing was left to make mulligan stew. Leaving the hobo, Tom and I started to follow the railroad north—we hoped.

We had walked for about an hour when we came to a farmhouse. Both of us were hungry and thirsty. Tom asked the lady if we could do some work for food. The lady said that she didn't have any chores but would be glad to feed us. I was flabbergasted when Tom told her that we would only take food if we worked for it, that we were taught not to be "beholden" to anyone. I couldn't believe Tom. I was perfectly willing to be "beholden" as hungry as I was. This lady found us some wood to chop and gave us a lot to eat.

This was the start of not being beholden that Tom held on to all the way north and afterward. It wasn't long until I was the same way. The lady asked us lots of questions that we didn't answer as we might be sent home. We just said we were going home as soon as we made enough money.

About noon that day we hopped our first freight train. We saw it on a side track waiting for another train to pass. As it started moving we climbed up the ladder and rode on top of the freight car. We were both really scared, and as it reached full speed the wind was cold. We were glad when it stopped. We climbed off hoping to get warmed up and eat. Seeing some hobos under the trestle with a small fire and a small kettle of the ever-present mulligan stew, we went over. Since we didn't have anything to add to the pot, and they didn't have much, we wasn't really welcome.

When we were warmed up some, Tom said, "Let's get something for the pot." Again we found a nearby farmhouse and asked to trade work for food. We chopped wood for awhile and got lots of things for the pot including a large piece of side meat. When we got back to the hobo camp it was almost dark. Seeing what we had brought,they really welcomed us this time. They were happy with the meat, saying that was something that would stick to your ribs.

The farm wife had questioned us about sleeping. We admitted that we were sleeping in the open and she gave us a blanket. Tom insisted that we chop more wood to pay for it. For my part, I was getting a little tired of this business about not being "beholden." I would easily have accepted without chopping more wood.

After we were full of stew, everyone felt better. They asked about where we were from and where we were going. Tom told them that we had no home and that we were heading north to the logging camps where they were hiring young boys to help the cooks. The hobos were helpful in telling us what rail lines led directly to Pennsylvania.

The next morning we ate more stew, then crawled into one of the rail cars, hoping it was going north. If not, we could jump off before it gathered up speed.

The train had gone about twenty miles and was stopped by railroad detectives, making all the hobos get off. By this time we were getting hungry again. We washed up in a creek the best we could, finger combing our hair. Stopping by another farmhouse, Tom again asked to do some work for food. We were offered food free as the lady had no chores. When Tom explained that we couldn't accept charity, I was mad enough to fight. Who was he to set such high standards for me when at that moment all I wanted was food—high standards could come later.

The lady found us some chores to do while she cooked a big dinner. She asked a lot of questions but was so nice and friendly that we didn't mind. We almost wished that she would adopt us. She offered us money, which of course Tom refused, but he did accept a towel and comb so we could make a better and cleaner appearance for the next place we stopped at. Before we left, she also gave us some advice. She said to Tom, "When you stop at the next place, let your brother do the asking. He's younger, skinnier, looks hungry, and will just melt them with those big brown eyes and that big smile." Then she gave Tom some advice which I loved to hear. She said, "Don't always insist that you have to work to pay for everything anyone does for you. You may be taking away the pleasure they get from helping. Even though you boys worked for your dinner, I will never forget cooking for two hungry little boys who are on their way to being successful in life."

We kept going north toward Pennsylvania, a few miles at a time, stopping to work a little for food and even money. The weather was warmer and it was getting to be a little like a vacation. We used the farm lady's advice, cleaning up and combing our hair before asking for work. Tom allowed me to be the one to ask for work. I learned to use the advice she had given me about looking people in the eye and smiling a lot. Tom even relented enough to sometimes accept small favors without paying for them with work. He finally began to realize that a lot of people liked to help two small boys for the pleasure it gave them.

After a few weeks we were in the very northern part of Virginia. We began to inquire about where to go in Pennsylvania to find where the timber was being cut and found that a big part of the work had moved into southern West Virginia. We followed the B & O Railroad into West Virginia until we found the timber camps.

Whole mountains of timber were being cut. We found logging camps, sawmills, and new railroads being built to haul out the timber. There was so much, so many things we had never even dreamed about.

There was all kinds of work available. Mostly for boys our age it was to help the cooks. The only problem was that most camps needed only one cook's helper and we wanted to stay together.

Finally we found two camps in Tucker County which were close together, both needing cook's helpers. I got a job at one and Tom at the other. The camps were about three miles apart.

The cook was the first one up in the morning, long before daylight. I was up with him building fires, setting tables and serving the food. How those men would eat—ham, eggs, biscuits, pancakes and even pie for breakfast. They would eat and be in the woods before daylight. A good cook was king of the camp, a poor one was run off. These hard-working men would only work in camps with a good cook.

Living in a logging camp was an experience to be remembered: a big room filled with bunk beds, heated with a big potbellied stove, and filled with the sounds of snoring all night long. Sometimes when bedbugs invaded the bunks, cursing would be added to the night sounds. The mattresses would have to be removed and treated. This was one of my jobs.

Surrounding the camp was the magnificent virgin forest of evergreen trees which seemed to reach the sky. Underneath the trees the floor of the forest was almost dark on a sunny day. All around me were the big trees, big logs, big horses, and big rough men. I was overwhelmed and lonely without Tom.

I was very young even for a cook's helper. The cook was a gruff and rough-talking man, as were most of the cooks in these camps. He kept me on the run as there was so much work to be done. I was so busy during the day that I didn't have time to get lonesome, but at night I would cry a little before going to sleep.

I soon found that the cook had a heart as big as his talk was rough. He let me sleep in his shack, away from the snoring and the bedbugs, always saving me the best of everything to eat.

One of the fascinating things in the camps were

the storytellers. I could've listened for hours. The truth, the lies, the funny stories, the scary stories: what great descriptive storytellers they were.

I had been encouraged in school to write. I liked this but found it very difficult to find anything interesting to write about. Now I had so many interesting stories, I decided to keep a diary. I would write every morning and afternoon, writing on every piece of paper I could find, so when I saw Tom, I would be able to remember all the stories I had heard and everything that had happened.

My diaries began to accumulate in the shack I shared with the cook. Sometimes he would pick one up, read it and grumble, "If that is about Joe Helm for gosh sake tell something about him. Joe is not just a name—he's different. Say so." I began to describe my storytellers as I saw them. One day the cook slammed a new composition book in front of me saying, "Boy, use this book for your scribbling. Everything I pick up has been written on." Coming from him, I knew this was a great compliment. When the book was filled a new one was there with the cook saying, "At least you won't be writing on the walls."

I took the cook's advice and described the storytellers exactly as I saw them. I knew he read magazines and books, but never dreamed he was reading the stories I wrote. Then one day I was shocked when he said, "Boy, them ornery woodhicks you couldn't fill with a number 4 shovel, are not ten feet high like you make them sound." I thought about this for a while, re-read some of my diaries, and decided to me they were ten feet tall, the strongest men in the world. They can do the most work, figure out how to do anything, tell the tallest tales, and I was willing to swear they could out eat any equal number of men in the world.

The cook may have been right, but not to a small boy barely 11 years old. I stayed in a state of awe and wonder at everything around me. To me the horses were larger and stronger than elephants. The trees reached the sky, and underneath was a carpet of moss three feet thick and so soft to walk through. I would sit under the giant evergreen trees and listen to the winds which had come three thousand miles to make music through the leaves and limbs. I liked to think that they were playing tunes just for me.

I worried sometimes when I wrote about the forest being cut. I had never heard of Paul Bunyan. If I had I would have been sure that my men were fully his equal and that they were sure to cut all the timber in the country in a few years. I wrote what I felt and it was of no concern or interest to anyone else but my diary and me. Well maybe the cook might look at something and make a gruff suggestion or two.

Suddenly things changed for me. I now had a helper. No one had ever heard of a cook's helper having a helper. The men teased me a little. I was worried a little that a new boy was being trained to replace me. I tried to work harder. I couldn't ever leave my heroes. When the cook saw that I was worried he said, "Boy, don't worry, you will be here as long as I am. I want you to get out more and learn what is going on."

Other things began to change also. All of the men treated me almost like a camp pet. All at once though two of the older men began to take a special interest in me, almost like they had decided to adopt me. One of them, Henry Shaffer, had been a school teacher and farmer. He lived a few miles from the camp and had several children of his own. He went to work in the woods, making a lot more money than he did when teaching. He was a log scaler. This was the man who measured the logs the men cut, as they were paid by the number of board feet in the logs cut. Mr. Shaffer began to give me lessons in the evenings. He was impressed that I knew so much math. He encouraged me by promising to train me to scale logs at higher wages.

The other man who more or less adopted me was Clarence Miller. He was an older man about sixty years old. It was said that Mr. Miller didn't work directly for the lumber company. Instead, he owned all of the teams that hauled the logs out of the woods, and was paid by the day for the use of his horses. Someway the teamsters worked for Mr. Miller, but were fed and housed by the company. Not long after Mr. Miller took an interest in me, he had me bring Tom to camp and offered him a job cleaning stable and feeding horses. He promised to teach Tom all about teams and the work. Again, Tom and I were together and it felt like we had two extra fathers.

I still never quite understood why I had suddenly became almost special in camp, even acquiring two fathers.

Then one Sunday evening a timberman came in from having the day off. He had come to work a couple of weeks before from another camp. He threw a weekly newspaper on the dining table and I started reading. I saw a story in it written by Johnny Lane. I thought, "Golly, someone has the same name as I do." The story was just like the one I had written in my diary. I went running for my diary. I had written so much, but I finally found the story written word for word the same as the one in the paper. It was hard to believe. When I asked the cook he said I'd have to wait and talk to Mr. Shaffer who had gone home.

When Mr. Shaffer came back he had me to meet with him in the cook's shack along with the cook and Mr. Miller. He first apologized to me, saying, "Johnny, the cook here started reading the diaries that you left laying around everywhere. He is a well-educated man and reads a lot. He had me read your diaries because he thought they were special. When I read them I thought they were special also."

He went on to tell me that was when the cook bought composition books for me to keep my diaries in. Then he told me that he copied all of my diaries and gave some of them to a newspaper editor and that was how my story got in the paper. He said that no one ever told me for fear that I would be embarrassed and quit keeping my diary. He got me to promise to keep writing.

He said that this meant so much to the men. He said that most of them had read what had been published and saved everything as it was a story about themselves seen through the eyes of a small boy. Maybe they weren't ten feet tall but they would always be proud that one small boy thought so. The men could now show the stories to their families to explain their lives in camp and the work they did.

Tom was now in camp with me working for Mr. Miller, who was teaching him about horses and how to care for them. The weather was getting colder. It was November. I was homesick, but not near as much since Tom was in camp with me.

A couple of months before, I had written in my diary "Going Home For Christmas." It appeared in the same paper. It was about going home to see my family along with Tom. I was dreaming that we might have enough money to go in style by riding the train in coaches and not in boxcars. I also dreamed that we would take our little brothers and sisters gifts. They had never seen anything but homemade toys. I dreamed that Tom and I might take fifty dollars if we could save it. Or even twenty-five dollars which would mean that the family could eat big the rest of the winter.

When I heard about this part of my diary appearing in the paper, I felt naked and embarrassed. I went to Mr. Shaffer and swore that I wouldn't write again. Mr. Shaffer said, "You can't let your friends in camp down." I said, "How would I be letting them down?" He told me, "They have read the story and are making plans for the train trip, and toys for your family. They are real excited, like it was their first Christmas, so don't let them down." I guess that I was easy to convince because I was so homesick.

Tom was another problem. When Mr. Miller wanted to send some money as a gift to the family, Tom said he couldn't accept it without working for it. Mr. Miller asked me for an answer. I told him how Tom didn't like to be "beholden," and suggested having Tom work extra to pay back the money. Mr. Miller then had Tom take courses by mail to learn to be a veterinarian. He could pay back the money by "doctoring" the teams. Tom and Mr. Miller became close friends.

The men seemed almost as excited as we were about our trip home. They had made a lot of toys for our brothers and sisters and had also bought toys to send. They gave us nearly one hundred dollars to take along. Tom objected to this as we hadn't earned this money. The men had Tom sit down along with me and "laid it on the line," saying in effect, "This is none of your business, this is a gift to your family from us, will you take it along or do we have to send it to your family?" Tom had to agree.

We were on our way by train. We rode in the coach this time and not as hobos, but first class.

We arrived at the train station nearest to our home but still several miles away. Our visit was to be a surprise so no one was there to meet us. We had a lot of gifts so we had to go to the livery stable and hire a man to take us home in a buggy.

We looked forward to surprising the family and did we ever surprise them. We felt like returning heroes. For a family that were usually embarrassed by shows of emotion, no one held back, except the younger ones. It took a little while for them to realize that we were their brothers. Even our father kept hugging us. We couldn't believe this.

Then we began to bring the gifts in the house all wrapped up with names on them. They couldn't be unwrapped until Christmas Day. They had to wait two more days. Were any five children more excited! They had never seen store-bought toys or clothes.

Every gift had a name on it. All of the hand-made toys told who it was from along with a letter from the person who gave the gift and why it was made for that particular brother or sister. Usually the reason given was because they had a boy or girl or brother or sister the same age. The next two days was spent shaking boxes and imagining what was inside them.

Finally the younger five were sent to bed. This gave Tom and I a chance to give our parents the money we had brought, nearly one hundred dollars. This was more money than they normally saw in a year. We knew our father was like Tom, he couldn't take something for nothing. We had a story ready that Tom was working extra for this money. I wasn't quite ready with an answer when Father asked what I was doing for my part of the money. The only thing I could think of was to get out my newspaper clippings and say I had been paid for them. This was somewhere near the truth, and by this time he got so interested in the articles that he forgot to quiz me further. Every so often he would shake his head and say, "You wrote this?" He could hardly believe this and neither could Mother.

The next morning I went to see Mr. Hays, my old school teacher. I guess I just had to show off a little, so I took my clippings along. He greeted me warmly and read them. He was really pleased when I told him that he was the one caused me to want to write and taught me how to write. Mr. Hays said, "I will take credit for encouraging you to write, but I can't take credit for your gift with words. Maybe you were born with that and I only recognized that."

Mr. Hays then told me that my sister, Mary Jane who was one year younger than me, really had a way with words and to encourage her to write. This gave me an idea. I had been wondering how to thank the men who had sent the gifts and made the toys in some special way. Maybe Mary Jane could write them a thank you letter. Although I wasn't convinced that she could do it, I would ask her. Tom and I had always been close and being the oldest I guess we felt a little superior to the younger ones, thinking of them as little nuisance "tag alongs."

The next day was Christmas. The family received more gifts than they ever expected to get in a lifetime. The homemade toys and games created great excitement and it seemed a million questions were asked. Each one had to know all about the person who made them a gift. I was sure glad I had the clippings. Most of the men who had sent gifts were described in my stories.

I had asked Mary Jane the day before to write a thank you letter to the men in the camp, telling her what the teacher had said about her ability to write. It almost scared her. She was sure the teacher was wrong and she couldn't write the letter. After Mary Jane saw all the gifts and read the clippings she told me that she just had to thank them, so she would write them.

A week later when we went back to camp I took her letter with me. It read:

Dear Men of the Mountains,

I am writing to thank you for helping to make this the greatest week in the life of me and my brothers and sisters.

First our brothers Tom and John came riding up in a buggy with all of the gifts you sent. Seeing our brothers after we had almost given up hope of ever seeing them again was gift enough to do us forever.

Then it got better because of all the gifts you made or bought for us—gifts that we hadn't ever dreamed of or never seen.

Then we got to read about you from the diaries John wrote. We also made my brothers tell us about every one of you who sent gifts. After they answered about a thousand questions, I think that the presents are not just presents but gifts from God, and that the gifts are sacred.

I will always remember "The Men of The Mountains" and hope someday to meet all of you. When I get older, I plan to leave home to work and go to school to be a teacher. Maybe then I will get to meet you.

From a little girl in the hills
Mary Jane Lane

When we got back the men had to know all about our trip, the family and how everyone liked their gifts. Much of this was answered in our little sister's letter. From our stories and my diaries she came to see them as giants of the earth, just like Tom and I. The men would read this letter over and over. They knew they were plain rough, hard-working men, yet they were so pleased that at least one little girl believed them to be special. Tom answered more questions while I told them I would write details in my diary for them to read.

By this time I knew that I could put my feelings on paper where I would be embarrassed to tell them. I filled in a few details about the trip home for Christmas that Tom and our sister's letter missed, but mostly I wrote about our coming north for work. On the trip home and then back I saw the places Tom and I had stopped when we came north the first time. I wrote in my diary as I saw it. Two little boys who had left home to find work. It had been a little rough at times, we had been a little hungry at times and a little cold. With the trip to refresh my memory I told of the people who had helped us and where they lived, and that Tom and I both planned to revisit and thank them. I told of the times we almost starved because Tom had refused to be "beholden," always making sure that our work was worth more than the food we ate.

Our sister's letter and my stories of the trip were published. The stories caused a lot of interest. I even got a lot of letters, many of them saying they had shed tears because of two young boys going through all this. This surprised me since by now I looked back on this as a great adventure to always be remembered.

The men in the camp read the part about Tom and said, "That's the old man, that's the old man." By now everyone call Tom "The Old Man" because of him being so serious with his medical studies and work with horses. He was still independent about taking something unless he earned it.

Mr. Shaffer went home for a weekend and came back with a letter for me. It was from his little girl. I had almost forgotten about her telling me she planned to marry me. In the letter she told me how she had read my story and cried, promising me that I would never get hungry or cold after we were married. When I showed her father he just laughed and advised me to leave the country if I wanted to escape.

By this time Tom and I both had sponsors, or teachers, and maybe adopted fathers. Mine was of course Mr. Shaffer, who loved to teach. I was his only pupil. He helped with my grammar and the three R's. He always encouraged me to keep writing my diary which by now was often a newspaper column. He said I had the gift of words, and started writing to my sister Mary Jane encouraging her to keep writing. He told her he could help find a high school/college where she could work for her education.

Mr. Miller continued to tutor and work with

Tom. He had Tom taking correspondence courses in veterinarian medicine, as well as working with him and other men who were experienced in doctoring animals. He planned that Tom would go back to school and maybe get a degree. He talked to Tom about a scholarship, and later I found out that Mr. Miller planned to finance this. This was to be unknown to Tom, since he still couldn't take something for nothing. I always wondered how Mr. Miller could have convinced Tom that a scholarship was not something for nothing.

Suddenly our world was shattered: Mr. Miller died with a heart attack. We both felt like we had lost a father. We had never lost anyone close to us before.

We attended his funeral along with Mr. Shaffer. We came back to camp certain that life would never be the same. We were right, but not in any manner we could imagine.

By now we were trained to make a living so we didn't have to worry about that. I was fourteen and Tom was fifteen. I could scale timber and was almost big enough to cut timber. Tom was almost an expert with horses and teams.

A day or so after Mr. Miller's funeral, Mr. Shaffer left for several days and we both really felt lost. When he returned he asked us both to go with him to the county seat on important business. He borrowed a buggy for the twenty-mile trip to a lawyer's office.

Tom and I had no idea what the important business was all about, except that Mr. Shaffer said it concerned Mr. Miller's will.

When the will was read it certainly did concern us and almost beyond our comprehension. It read on and on, but basically said Mr. Miller, a bachelor, had been an orphan and had no living relatives, had left the bulk of his estate to Tom and I. Mr. Shaffer was left ten percent and was given power of attorney until Tom and I reached age twenty-one.

The will listed the property he owned, assets in the bank, as well as the teams of horses being used in the timber operation where we were working now. We were now a long way from where we had started since camp sites were moved as the timber was all cut in one area.

All of this was almost beyond my comprehension. I now had inherited a lot of property but didn't know what it all meant. Tom and I now owned all the teams of horses, but what did it mean? The horses didn't seem to notice or seem much impressed. They still needed to be fed, watered, stabled and cared for the same as ever, and Tom and I worked the same as ever.

This had to change before long. Mr. Shaffer began to take us to the courthouse. We now had to get a lawyer and see judges. Because we were minors we needed legal protection. The officials began to realize that a lot of valuable assets were involved. They all got a big laugh when Tom and I started worrying about losing wages because of all these meetings.

At this time Mr. Shaffer said, "Let's have a meeting, and I will explain everything I know about this business left to you by Mr. Miller."

Mr. Shaffer then explained that although the assets were enormous in potential, there was money to be made if managed right. A lot of money could be made by the teams of horses if we could hold Mr. Miller's contract with the lumber company. He explained that the big assets were in the form of timber property and a couple of adjoining farms. The one real big asset was one huge piece of property full of timber of several thousand acres. The drawback was that it could be years before a railroad came near this remote section.

He then said, "I am overwhelmed by this Power of Attorney and I need help. The help I need is for you boys to grow up in a hurry. We three will meet and discuss everything and make a decision together."

We then talked about an immediate problem, hiring a boss for the teamsters. We all agreed that Tom was too young to have the respect of the men. Not long before he had been the stable boy. We agreed to ask one of the older men to be superintendent. His name was Jim Feamster. He agreed to take the job. The men had long ago given him the nickname "Feamster the Teamster."

Mr. Shaffer also suggested that we get our father to move close so he could sign papers and maybe help with some decisions. When I asked if we had money to move the family, he laughed and said that Mr. Miller had to always keep many thousands of dollars in the bank to finance operations week to week, therefore it was no problem. He then reminded me that we now owned four farms including a nice home where Mr. Miller had lived. He suggested that they move into that house. He then teased me a little saying, "Since my little girl still plans to marry you, it will be a chance for her to meet your family."

I was chosen to go home to sell the family on the idea of moving to the farms up north. When I left for home I was armed with a certified check, a picture of the farmhouse and a newspaper story about Mr. Miller leaving everything to us. I wasn't sure anyone would believe me without this proof. I still wasn't sure that I wouldn't wake up and find that it was all a dream.

Tom and I had been back a few times since our first Christmas visit so it wouldn't be the unexpected visit our first trip had been. I was anxious about convincing the family to go back with me, so I spent time as I rode writing about the farm in the high mountains. I described the farm as only part of a large piece of virgin forest land with hemlock and spruce trees that stayed green the year around. I told how you could see almost forever from the high fields, and how the sun never shined on the ground underneath the evergreens as they were so thick. I also described how the animals, including bear and deer, would be in the fields at times. I wrote and wrote, hoping to convince the family that it would be a great place to live.

One day a well-dressed man was seated next to me. I was anxious to write and didn't talk much. I suppose he had been reading part of what I wrote and finally asked if he could read all of it. I said sure but asked if he would tell me whether it would convince my family to move. He not only pronounced it convincing but had me give him its location and pledged to visit someday. He said he especially wanted to see these mountains when they were covered with deep snow and the giant evergreen trees looked as if they were buried in snow along with the fields.

This input from the stranger gave me confidence that I could convince the family to move.

I finally arrived home. It wasn't as dramatic as our first trip, but still exciting. I waited until all of the greetings were over and the evening meal finished before I asked the family to sit and listen to what I had to say.

As I told of how Tom and I had left home, two little boys to find work, returning less that five years later wealthy, I could hardly believe the story myself. How could I convince the family when it seemed like a dream to me?

Still I plowed on with my story, telling them of the home that could be theirs if they would only move. I told Father how he could make a good living from the farm and working in the winter in the timber. All of my brothers and sisters were excited and ready to move the next day. The idea of taking their first train ride had a lot to do with their excitement.

My parents had very little to say, and I wondered if they believed me. It occurred to me that we hardly knew each other. I had left when I was ten and had only been back for a few days at a time. How could they really know me—one of eight children—when they had always worked long, long hours.

Finally I asked to talk to my parents alone while my sister Mary Jane took the younger children into the next room and read to them what I had written about their new home.

I sat at the table and got out all of the papers I had brought. First I showed them a picture of Tom and me standing in front of the house that would be theirs. Then I showed them a letter from Mr. Shaffer explaining how this had all come about. Then the newspaper articles telling about our inheritance. Last I showed them the certified check for one thousand dollars which was to be used for moving expenses. After the check and the letter from Mr. Shaffer telling how Father was needed to sign papers because of our age, they ended up almost as excited as the children. I decided to return back to the mountains and they would follow in a few days.

When I got back a lot more details were known than when I left. It seemed that Mr. Miller had foreseen the great boom in the timber industry. He had invested in teams of horses, hired teamsters and made contracts with the timbering companies to haul logs to the railroads. He had made a lot of money according to Mr. Shaffer. We now owned a lot of valuable timber. The only drawback was that most of it lay miles away with no railroads within miles. Mr. Shaffer explained that there were small tracts of timber closer with a lot of value. He said that we were already getting offers for this property, but even they would be of more value if we waited until the railroad came closer to timber.

We were being pressured to sell. The first offer came from the timber company who had a contract with us to haul logs. The owners lived in Boston.

They made an offer to buy all of the teams of horses at a much lower price than they were worth, hinting that the contract to haul logs from the woods would not be renewed if we didn't sell.

All of this was almost beyond our comprehension as Mr. Shaffer explained it to us. We had to depend on the judgement of him and Mr. Miller's lawyer now for our advice. They told us it was up to Tom and me. The assets could be sold for enough that we would be fairly wealthy, or we could work, keep everything and could go broke, or sometime be millionaire lumbermen. That decision was ours. Mr. Shaffer explained that we would have to grow up in a hurry as decisions like this would be continual, and he would not make them for us.

We decided to keep the business. Tom would stay and fulfill the contract along with Mr. Feamster. Mr. Shaffer and I quit working for the company. We immediately started traveling in the region contacting other logging companies about hiring our teams and teamsters.

Almost all of them knew about Mr. Miller and his teams. Surprisingly Tom had also gained a good reputation as a protégé of Mr. Miller's. Also, it seemed that everyone knew who I was through my diaries in the newspapers. Sometimes we stayed overnight in logging camps. There I was almost embarrassed by being treated like a hero because of my diaries.

We found that we would have little trouble getting other contracts for our men and teams. Before we even got back, word of our travel had gotten back to camp and to the owners. They had already sent a man down from Boston to offer us a new and better contract. We decided to re-sign with them.

Then our family came to their new home. To all of them the new home was special and almost beyond their dreams, even after my pictures and description. The children could hardly stop talking about the train ride and the trip to the farm by a rented carriage. Our parents were especially happy with the schools being nearby and the possibility of the children getting a higher education.

My father was especially thrilled by the farm. It still was stocked with cows, chickens, hogs and horses. Spring was only a few months away and he could hardly wait until he could plow and plant. He had always loved farming, but with a small hillside farm he had barely scratched out a living. Now he had a farm he could only dream about before.

It would be awhile before he could farm personally, because Tom and I needed, and came to depend on, his help as things kept moving and changing too fast. Tom, his teams and teamsters became the source of income without having to sell any of our land. It was left to me to handle the business, along with Mr. Shaffer and our lawyer. I was fifteen years old with no business experience. I felt totally alone and almost naked, but determined to hold on to everything Mr. Miller had left to us.

Mr. Shaffer was working full time for us now. He would say, "I can help with information but the final decisions will be yours, as Tom will be busy with filling the contracts."

Pressure was coming from everywhere to buy or steal our land. Since Father would have to sign every legal paper as we were minors, Mr. Shaffer and I would take him to the lawyers, the court-house, and everywhere so he could learn about the business.

At our lawyer's suggestion we formed a company called *The Land Logging and Lumber Company.* At fifteen years old, I was president, Tom was vice-president and Mr. Shaffer was secretary and trea-surer. Father was listed as a special vice-president who had to sign all legal papers until Tom and I were twenty-one. We had to all be educated togeth-er.

We had to learn where all the tracts of land were and their boundaries. Most of the boundaries were in dispute or overlapped. Many land speculators from New York, Boston or elsewhere had bought large tracts of land in the area years before. They would send surveyors in to mark corner trees. The trees might be a couple of miles away where some of the men would build a fire. The smoke from the fire would be used as a corner and marker. If the smoke from the fire was affected by the wind the marked corner would be wrong. Another company using the same method might cause the lines to overlap or not meet, resulting in many court cases and disputes.

Many times a large logging company would just ignore property lines and cut the timber on it. If the owner had very little money, he couldn't afford to file suit and lost his timber.

We soon had a test on this. A teamster who once worked for Mr. Miller came to Mr. Shaffer telling him that he was hauling logs from a tract of land that Mr. Miller had once told him that he owned. When we looked up the deeds and had it surveyed we found that our timber was being stolen. Our lawyer tried to get an injunction, which was fought by the company's high-priced lawyers.

Father offered a great idea, his first but by no means his last. By now, he had spent a lot of time with the teamsters, loggers and men that had read my diaries, taking great pride in what they said. He suggested that we go to the newspapers that had published my diaries and have them write a story about the stolen lumber. When we talked to the editor he couldn't wait to do a story and editorial blasting the logging company. He had already written about timber being cut on property owned by other settlers.

Did this ever cause an uproar! All the readers were mad. Our old friends among the loggers were ready to do battle. They were in a good position to take action. Many of them now worked for the logging company stealing the logs, quit and went to work for other logging companies. The company sent people to make a settlement for the timber they had cut and ran ads explaining how they had made a mistake.

Our father then suggested that we look up these tracts of timber, have them surveyed and the property marked with a special mark or paint. This would keep other logging companies from cutting our timber and then claiming they had made a mistake.

Father not only started having the tracts surveyed, but went with them to learn to survey land himself. This caused him to have a lot of mixed feelings as he wanted to farm. We finally found a person to work the farm for him, leaving him free to learn about our business. He proved invaluable as time went by. He would go to the courthouse and look up deeds, study maps, and ask questions of the lawyer and Mr. Shaffer.

Mr. Shaffer began asking me about Father's educational background saying that he had never been around anyone who grasped things or learned so fast.

The family settled in their new home, high up on the mountain. They loved it here with rooms almost as big as the whole cabin in West Virginia. They were all in school where Mr. Shaffer's children attended. My sister Mary Jane was in the eighth grade now and still loved to write. Her classmate and best friend was Mr. Shaffer's oldest daughter, Rose, the one that always said she planned to marry me.

By the next spring things had pretty well worked out so far as work was concerned. Tom's contracts had expanded to other logging companies and we now owned a lot more teams. The profits from this operation was now supporting all of us. This removed the pressure of having to sell timberland before it became more valuable as railroads came closer.

I was now sixteen years old and in charge of all other assets except that I still consulted with our father and never made a decision until we studied everything together.

As railroads were built farther and farther into the back country we did start to sell off some timberland, making sure all boundaries were checked first. Sometimes we would hire surveyors, but after working with them, Father and I learned to do this ourselves.

We also needed to learn the value of timber on each tract of land. Mr. Shaffer would go along with us at first because of his experience as a log scaler. He, of course, taught us a lot. This was different. These were trees, not cut logs that could be measured at each end and then multiplied by the length. This gave the board feet in an entire tract of land in order to know what a fair price might be.

In order to do this we would mark off a few select acres that were typical of the whole tract. Then we would select a few trees that looked like the average size, measure across and estimate the height. Thus we would then have an educated guess on the board feet average of several trees in one acre. Doing this in several selected acres and multiplying this by the number of acres in the tract, we would have our estimate of the value of the timber.

Father and I learned to enjoy looking up tracts of land this first winter working together. We were limited in the number of days we could go out in the high snowy mountains. We sure had plenty to do as we had much to learn.

A representative from one of the large lumber companies came to make an offer for a small tract of timber. By now I was the spokesman for our business deals. The representative seemed surprised to find himself talking to someone so young. I guess this led him to believe that it could be bought cheap. He referred to it as a little timber on a few acres on Deer Creek. I told him that he must be talking about some other land, that our land consisted of one hundred eighty-four acres and every acre had large trees. I said we would show him the property lines and he could have his people to estimate the amount of board feet of lumber in the tract. I don't think he believed me until his people came up with almost the same amount.

It was important that the people we hoped to deal with came to know that we knew the value of our holdings and not waste our time trying to get our land for a lot less than it was worth. We did sell this tract of timber and several others as railroads were built closer. This gave us a lot of money that we could reinvest.

When the weather got warmer in the spring, Mr. Shaffer, my father and I went to see the main tract of timber left to us by Mr. Miller. It lay nearly one hundred miles south in a very remote section of West Virginia. I had read among Mr. Miller's papers that this timberland would be a great long-term investment and he had bought nearly fifty thousand acres. The price had been very low because it was thought then that there would be no way of ever getting the timber out.

We looked up the courthouse records, hired a local surveyor and was able to tell almost where it all lay. Most of the timber was very much like the trees we worked with the exception that the evergreen trees were bigger and taller. I then told them my idea of selling our tracts back home and using the money to buy much lower-priced timberland adjoining this huge tract of land. I think they both believed that I was out of my mind.

Tom and I owned the company, but I trusted Father's and Mr. Shaffer's judgement and wanted their approval. So I explained to them that I believed that timber would be cut a lot sooner than people thought. I told them that I had bought books about timbering from Canada south through the New England states, New York and Pennsylvania. I had learned how they had floated thousands of logs on rugged rivers during floods. I also pointed out on maps the rivers that ran towards these mountains. Railroads could be easily built alongside the rivers' natural routes.

At least I convinced them to find a real estate agent to let us know when tracts of timber became for sale. Before we returned home the agent had us inspect several tracts that he thought might become available. In the next several years lots of land became available. Then the problem was how to raise enough money to buy the land. I also had the problem of convincing everyone that this wasn't too much of a gamble, but how could I convince everyone else when I wasn't sure myself?

Still we had small tracts of timber that became more valuable as the railroads came closer and the contracts that Tom handled became larger and more profitable. Almost all profits went into buying more tracts of timber adjoining this property. Since this was mostly my idea I stayed nervous from the pressure of the gamble.

By the time I was seventeen years old I found it was up to me to negotiate all deals. Of course, everything was discussed with my father and Mr. Shaffer before I bought or sold anything. I tried to shave an almost imaginary beard in order to look older, without much success.

Along with me, my brothers and sisters were getting older. So were Mr. Shaffer's children. They were neighbors to each other and friends, especially my sister Mary Jane and Rose Shaffer. Rose never wavered in her plan to marry me. It was accepted by everyone that we would marry someday, including me. I never saw a lot of Rose. Our relationship was still a little strange. It was more like—someday we will court and someday we will marry. Sometimes she would ask what subjects to study in order to help with our business.

We decided that she go on to school and study business finance and bookkeeping. In order to go to college, Rose had to board at a dormitory. We began to write. Looking back our letters must have been strange, two young people who planned to marry writing each other regularly but they seemed to be business letters rather than love letters.

Rose was always writing asking questions about business, how her courses connected with practical business. She was determined to take any course that might prove helpful. Mr. Shaffer suggested instead of finance and bookkeeping she should take business law or the nearest equivalent at the time. He also suggested that she find part-time work with a lawyer where most knowledge was learned at the time.

Rose came home for Christmas, but I missed her as I was away making a deal for timberland adjoining our land in the county south of us. We continued to write regularly but the tone of our letters changed a little. I began to notice some dry humor in her letters and she had always been so serious. I once wrote that all our letters seemed to be about business and she replied that she had found my letters to be very romantic. True they were not boy-and-girl romantic but romantic about the trees, the woods and the timbermen.

Then Rose came home for the summer. This time I couldn't wait to see her. It was worth the wait. How she had blossomed since last summer! She had gone away with a young girl's body and a young girl's mind and returned with a woman's mind and a woman's body. I was overwhelmed. I couldn't seem to stay away.

I was intrigued how this serious little girl had a great sense of humor. Of course, I just hadn't discovered it before. I finally realized that I was in love. How was I to tell someone that I had planned for years to marry, that I was now in love with her? Then it occurred to me. She had written to me that

I had indeed written romantic letters to her about the trees and everything, so I decided to write her a letter in story form.

I called it, "My Little Rose of The Mountain." I told how a rosebud had been promised to me long before I ever dreamed that it would become the most lovely flower in the hills. I told her how I now realized that my heroes, the men of the mountains, had to have wives and mothers. I mentioned her sense of humor that I had just discovered. From then on we had a great fun engagement. Rose told me how she had kept her sense of humor from me, thinking I might see it as silly.

Big things were happening in our business. We were approached by some land speculators. A small group without a lot of money had secured options on hundreds of thousands of acres of timberland about one hundred miles from our tract. They had gambled all of their assets believing that they could sell their options to larger timbering companies who were working their way south all the way from Canada.

This tract of land covered an entire river basin, with only one railroad within a hundred and fifty miles. The railroad was a few miles away but it ran up the New River Gorge. No one knew at that time whether a connecting railroad could be built to come up from the gorge to the hilltops. Therefore the group was having a hard time selling their options to big operators and they were getting desperate as their options would run out in another year.

The group came to us trying to sell the land. The whole deal was too big to even think about as all our assets were tied up in timberland. Still I could always dream about trees and timber. We had already bought most of the available land near our large tract. Maybe we could get smaller tracts from this huge section. I just had to see this timberland.

I contacted the leading member of this group by letter, telling him that I could only promise that we might be interested in only a few sections. The man's name was Joe Haynes. He invited me to go with him to see the miles of land. I think that he almost backed out of going with me when he saw how young I was. We traveled for several days looking at a lot of beautiful timber and land. The timber was big and beautiful, a lot more hardwoods, magnificent pine, spruce and hemlock.

Joe and I became pretty good friends in the two weeks we were together. He was impressed with my knowledge of timbering and ability to judge the amount of board feet per acre.

Joe had been a person who had gotten a lot of people to invest money into buying options on this vast acreage. The options were running out in a few months. Joe felt a lot of pressure from the investors who would lose their money. Between us we came up with a new idea. Maybe our company could buy these options from Joe's investors, who would just be happy to get their money back.

We would only be interested if Joe could go back to the land owners and buy new options from them. Joe was certain the owners would be willing to do this as they had been disappointed that no big timbering companies had showed interest in this area.

I was interested because I believed in two or three years some company much larger than ours would buy our options and we could make a good profit by reselling the options.

I told Joe he would be hearing from me as soon as we held a meeting. At the meeting everyone agreed to go ahead with the deal if it could be worked out and the new options remained reasonable. We put Joe Haynes on salary with authority to get options in our name. When I wanted Mr. Shaffer, my father and Tom to double check my judgement, they all insisted that they trusted my judgement. Since I was not quite eighteen years old, I took this as a great compliment.

I insisted that someone go back with me to see at least part of this acreage of hardwood forest. Mr. Shaffer agreed to ride with me. We agreed to ride horses so we could see as much as possible in just a few days. He was so impressed that we rode for two weeks, seeing more and more of this huge hardwood forest.

Joe rode with us part of the time. He had already talked to a lot of the owners about renewing their leases and had very favorable responses.

We returned home taking Joe with us. Since we had hired Joe to work for us with authority to buy options, our lawyers drew up a lot of blank options for him to work with. He began to send in options so fast, we had to set up a local bank account so that he could close the deals immediately.

Our original operation was still a great money maker. The profits had mostly gone to buy the evergreen forests one hundred miles south with little prospects that it could be transported to market for a few years yet. Now that our extra profits were going to buy options on a river drainage area of timber, we decided to recall our options at a profit.

The options were tough to sell. Everyone was interested in all of the timber, but concerned that it might be years, if ever, before a railroad could reach it. Most of them were not interested in long term investments. The river was too small to float logs.

Meanwhile, Rose was turning into a real jewel. Much more than just a beautiful woman but also a real asset in the timber business. She went to work for a lawyer who had spent forty years in the buying and selling of land. Soon she was knowledgeable about every phase of the business.

When I asked her to set a wedding date she said, "We will wait until we can settle in one place. Besides your number one marriage is still to the big timber." I talked to Rose about every phase of our business until she grasped everything along with her knowledge of the law.

I kept calling on the largest timber companies, trying to sell the timber options. A lot of people were interested but said either "not yet" or thought it was too big to handle.

Rose told me about a letter the lawyer she worked for had received. It was from a large lumber company with headquarters in Boston asking about timber in West Virginia. Inquiring we found that they had started cutting timber in Canada and had worked their way south through Pennsylvania. Now they were ready to move into West Virginia.

I wrote and asked for an appointment to meet the president of this company at his office in Boston. They replied giving me the appointment with the president, Mr. Byers.

I arrived for the appointment all dressed up but not feeling very comfortable—more like a hog in a bow tie. Mr. Byers was nice but looked very shocked to see an eighteen-year-old in his large fancy office. As I explained about the options we owned on the timberland, he began to ask questions more out of curiosity than anything else. What was this young kid doing here trying to sell options to land that he even wondered if I had the right to sell. He asked a test question: "Where does this land lay?" I showed him a large map of West Virginia and pointed out details and described the timber, and gave him an estimate of the board feet per acre and the lay of the land. He wanted to know how I knew all of this. I explained that I had rode all over this land myself. He then wanted to know how I learned to estimate timber like this. I told him how Tom and I had gone to work in timber camps, with Mr. Shaffer teaching me how to scale timber and estimate board feet on standing timber.

I had written him under the letterhead of *T and J Lumber Company*. He asked what the T and J stood for and I told him that the T was for my brother Tom and the J was for me, John. Then he asked why our company wasn't interested in developing some of this land. I explained how all of our money was in the land we had bought in the headwaters of the Greenbrier and Cheat rivers. This almost brought him out of his chair. "You own land where?" When I showed him on the map where and how much, he stared at me in disbelief. He asked me to stay overnight and come in the next morning to see him.

The next morning Mr. Byers greeted me warmly. He said, "John, I asked you all those questions yesterday because I was intrigued by you and your story. I was curious and interested more in your story than in the land. I had you leave the office so I could check with our representative in West Virginia to see what they could find out about your company. The telegraph company must be rich after all of the information I received already calling you a legend in the timber industry." Mr. Byers had me stay in Boston for a week while he received all copies of stories I had written years ago. He became my friend instantly because his own story was also like ours.

Before I left he told me why he nearly jumped out of his chair when I mentioned owning timber at the head of the Greenbrier and Cheat rivers. A huge lumber mill was now being built at the lower end of the river, and a number of Canadian lumber companies were interested in timber in this area. They already had enough men to float logs downriver at flood stage.

Over a period of two or three years the land became very valuable. We sold it to Mr. Byers' company for far more than enough money to buy up all the land we had options on. In a few more years we built a huge mill and started our own town called Lanesville.

By this time Rose and I were married as was

Tom and my sister Mary Jane. Maybe someday my sister and I will write the history of Lanesville.

Photographs Courtesy of Dan Snyder

THE OLD TRAINS

Photographs Courtesy of Dan Snyder

UP ON THE MOUNTAIN

Photographs by John Killoran
Courtesy of Dan Snyder

THE TEACHER

His name was James Cramer. He became my teacher when I was twelve years old and attending a one-room, mountain school. I had had two teachers before Mr. Cramer and several others after him. Many of them were good teachers, maybe special teachers, but, in retrospect, Mr. Cramer became "The Teacher." Through the years he has remained in my mind and heart "The Teacher," the greatest influence in my early life.

I was born the last of five children to Mike and Molly Conner, almost as an afterthought. I was what my mother called a change-of-life baby. She was a hard-working woman, whether by choice or necessity I don't know. My father was a hard-drinking lumberjack who left the burden of the farm and children to her. I am sure my coming when her first four children were half-grown was not a happy event, but she was a loving mother. However, she was not given to showing affection openly.

Tim and Susan were the brother and sister I remember most from my early childhood. Susan helped Mom with the housework and with me while Mom and Tim gardened and farmed our small plot of land there in the mountains of southern West Virginia. Mother raised the garden, took care of the animals, canned the produce, wove and sewed our clothes. Tim furnished fresh meat for the table by hunting wild game and earned extra money by trapping animals and selling the furs. We were fairly well sustained without much help from our father since he lived most of the time at the lumber camp and drank up most of his pay.

Tim began to take me hunting and fishing with him when I was big enough to tow the equipment. I can see myself trying to keep up with Tim while carrying fishing poles which were taller than I was.

A very old man, Mr. Johnson, was our nearest neighbor. He taught Tim hunting and fishing skills, and Tim taught me. He also taught Tim about the land, nature and the habits and instincts of the animals which lived in the woods around us.

When I was older I went alone to see Mr. Johnson. He was old and crippled, but he seemed to enjoy our talks as much as I did. On our walks he would talk for hours about the plants, flowers and trees we saw. He told about how to hunt and trap animals, and later he would quiz me to find out how much I remembered. It pleased him that I told him in almost his own words what he had told me.

I heard him tell my mother once, "Most folks go through life looking but never seeing. When your youngin', Charles, looks at something, he looks and sees too; then he remembers." I felt ten feet tall when he praised me like that.

It was the darkest day of my young life when Mr. Johnson died.

Much to my disgust, I was forced to start school when I was seven. Even though I could walk for miles through the woods, I insisted that I was too young to walk two miles to our one-room school. My parents didn't buy any argument. I was not interested in book learning. For the first few years I had a teacher who cared as little as I did as long as he collected his pay. Still I learned some things due to Susan's after-school tutoring. Mother backed her up. I thought it was a terrible waste of time to be penned up in the house when I could have been in the woods.

Tim married when I was ten years old and moved to his own farm, so now I was the farmer, hunter and trapper for the family. Mother insisted that these tasks should not interfere with my schooling. Neither Mother nor Father could read or write, and Mother wanted more for her children.

About this time a new teacher came to our school, and he was so much better than the other one that, in spite of myself, I began to like to learn, but the outdoors was still my main interest. I was beginning to be known as a good trapper and hunter, and I earned money by selling furs to the country store. I turned over all my money to mother. She never told father about the extra cash in the house for fear he would take it and spend it for liquor.

My life went along like this until Mr. Cramer came into our neighborhood to teach school. He was my third teacher. He was really interested in the students and wanted us to learn. During the summer months he was a timberman, but he was a teacher the rest of the year. He was a natural born teacher and stirred my interest from the first day he was there. I don't think I impressed him at all until the day I disagreed with the book he was using to teach another older class about nature and wild animals. From my experiences with trapping, fishing and hunting (I was only twelve), I butted in and said my piece. He looked at me, asked a question or two and quietly asked me to stay after school. I thought I had asked for trouble and was going to be punished.

As the other students left, some of them gave me a pitying look. Mr. Cramer sat down with me and talked about the books, nature, animals, hunting, trapping and fishing. He asked me why I had disagreed with the book. I told him about Tim's and Mr. Johnson's teachings of nature and how I had added to their knowledge with observations of my own. He seemed impressed with my recall of Mr. Johnson's words after all the years which had passed. He suggested that we go on "field trips" so we could share our knowledge. The next day we started on the first of our many field trips. Often he would bring special books with him. I began to be interested in reading for learning instead of just having to read because it was schoolwork. He explained that my knowledge of plants and animals was limited to my region, and differences could be due to food supply, weather, water, geological differences, etc. He didn't talk down to me, and he seemed to be impressed with my retentive memory.

As time went on, my teacher began to tell me of interesting things in books in other subjects, and he loaned me books for many subjects. He would say, "Charles, you have the gift of a good memory and the ability to understand what you read. Don't throw it away."

As we hunted, fished and took long walks I learned he had grown up in the mountains as I had, had gone through the eighth grade, and then he had taken a teacher's test. He loved teaching and regretted he had never had more schooling. He bought books and studied on his own, earning the nickname of "The Professor" in the lumber camp where he worked during the summer to supplement his income. He said his ambition was to have one of his students go to college—and I was the one.

Me? A poor mountain boy in college? I could as soon see myself on the moon. When I recovered from my shock I found he was serious about this. Over the next few months he began to challenge me to study harder and in a wider field of subjects.

Slowly I responded to his challenge and began to believe in his dream for me. It was hard going because of my necessary duties at home, schooling during the day and studying at night. It took several years before he was satisfied I could even think of applying to a college. By that time I knew I had to compete because of Mr. Cramer's challenge and his belief in me.

Mr. Alexander Smith, the owner of a large logging company, and a rich man by my standards, came to our area to fish and hunt. He hired me to guide him to the best areas of our county for these sports before my last year of attending the one-room school. I was with him for nearly two weeks, and he was impressed with my knowledge of the woods, the animals and fishing lore. Around the campfire at night we talked, and I told him of my plans for college. I told him I was going to succeed because of my teacher, Mr. Cramer, who had influenced my life so much.

Mr. Smith was real quiet for awhile, as though making up his mind to do something. Maybe he thought this was a wild story. Finally he said he would like to talk with my teacher before he left. He said he might have an idea.

When he talked with Mr. Cramer he told him that if he could get me admitted to a certain college in the foothills of Kentucky he would write a friend in that town who might find me a place to stay where I could work for room and board. Mr. Smith later wrote Mr. Cramer to tell me who to see at the college as at least some work could be furnished.

Early in September I was on my way to Buford College in Kentucky. Much to my surprise, my mother gave me money she had saved from the money I had always turned over to her. I had most of the clothes I owned on my back. The balance was bundled up in what we called a "turkey." I had to walk ten miles to catch a train so I could ride the rest of the way.

I arrived in the little town of Buford about four o'clock that evening and made my way to the address I had been given by Mr. Cramer. He had also given me a lot of last-minute encouragement.

A woman with gray hair, who looked to be about seventy years old, answered the door. When I told her my name, she looked shocked at my appearance. I didn't blame her. I had on the only coat, shirt and trousers I owned, and they were home-made, mountain styled and badly out of date. I was six feet tall and weighed 120 pounds. I was still dirty from the long trip, even though I had washed my hands and face on the train.

She said that her name was Ruby Ellis, but everyone called her "Grandma." She invited me in and showed me my room, a little bit reluctantly it seemed to me, but I couldn't blame her.

We talked, and she told me that I could have a room for chopping firewood and doing other chores. She said I would have to eat elsewhere as she was a widow and had very little income. I was expected to help her with the chickens and to milk the cow she owned. She cooked for both of us that evening.

She asked me if I had a change of clothes to wear when I went to register the next day. When I told her that this was all I owned, she asked me to go to my room and put my clothes outside the door. She cleaned them some and also pressed them. The next morning she gave me a breakfast of eggs, bread and a glass of milk.

That morning I went to see the registrar at Buford College. Neither he nor other teachers around the office seemed to believe what they were seeing and hearing when I talked. My West Virginia dialect was much different from theirs. They questioned me about my scholastic back-ground. There was some head-shaking. I was asked to leave the room for a few minutes. Then I was told I would have to take an entrance examination, which was arranged. After the tests I received some more odd looks, but I was told I was accepted. My registration fee was seventeen dollars. Mr. Cramer had told me about this, but I was shocked.

I had saved about four hundred dollars, but how could this last for four years? I might not be able to earn much money during the summer months. I asked about work so I could earn my meals, but all of the jobs were taken by upper class people.

The registrar asked me to come back when his workday was over to talk with him. He told me that he had known my teacher years before and had only agreed to accept me because of Mr. Cramer's letters. He said he still couldn't have accepted me unless I passed the entrance examination the other officials had demanded. My test results had solved that problem. He said I did well on the subjects I had never had in school, but Mr. Cramer had prepared me well. Mr. Cramer had never had those subjects in school either. In the other basic subjects I had made almost perfect scores.

We again talked about my food situation. When I told him about Grandma Ellis and her lack of money for food, he made a few suggestions, telling me how many other students had managed and giving me valuable ideas to try.

I went back to Grandma Ellis and asked her if any time I furnished food she would cook for both of us. She said, "I'd just love to do that."

There was nearly one week before school started. The next morning I set out for the farms outside town, asking for work and agreeing to take produce instead of wages. At the third farm they were digging potatoes and were glad to exchange produce for labor. I worked hard and was fed twice at the farmhouse that day. I came back to Grandma Ellis's house with a full stomach, all the produce I could carry and an old pair of overalls for work clothes. I set the sack down and said, "Grandma, we eat tonight." She nearly cried. She said it was good to have someone to cook for, as well as to have something to cook. I was full as a tick, but I ate again to keep her from having a broken heart.

By this time she had broken me from calling her Mrs. Ellis. The rest of the week I brought her quite a supply of produce and other food we could keep longer, such as flour and meal.

The farmer I worked for that week, Mr. McGraw, became my friend and helped me find work with other farmers who needed help. He would also tell me who not to work for as they might not pay me as much as I deserved. That whole fall he found so much work for me when I had spare time that I had brought in enough food to last for several months. Grandma kept canning vegetables.

I brought a supply of hay and corn for the cow and the chickens. We would all eat for awhile.

My first day at college was, for me, both high school and college. I had bought used textbooks, a pencil, notebook and paper. I had studied the books some before classes started. The other students stared at me and laughed when I talked. My tall, skinny body, my crude clothes and my dialect were a source of amusement to them. I picked up a wide range of nicknames. Even though all of the students were from rural areas and many were from the hills, I soon became the "Hillbilly." My dialect was different from that of the other students and was strange to them. I soon became well known, but this was hardly a compliment. At least I was a source of entertainment, which made me more determined to show them what a dumb hillbilly could do in the classroom.

I was really lonesome for home and for my teacher, Mr. Cramer. He wrote me every week and encouraged me. I longed for my mountains, my hunting dogs and the woods—the miles and miles of woods where I knew every mountain and valley, and almost every tree. I didn't make any close friends for a long time as I was busy working for farmers and studying every night.

Grandma was a real source of joy. We would talk at the supper table and then wash the dishes together before she went to bed.

I would study in the kitchen by a kerosene lamp. She didn't think it was "man's work" for me to help do the dishes, but she got to liking it as I wanted to hear her stories, and she enjoyed telling them.

After months in college I was still a great source of amusement to the other students and almost corrupted the dialect of some of them. My words and expressions were mocked so much that these strange words almost became a part of the local speech.

Sometime during the year I picked up another nickname that I didn't know about until someone told me a year or so later. It started with a professor in an English grammar class. After he asked a question of the better students in class and did not get a correct answer, he would always turn to me and say, "Well, Charles?" I usually knew the answer. Behind by back I was called "Well, Charles." No one ever called me "Well, Charles" to my face.

When the first six weeks tests came back my grades were just average in the two subjects I had never studied before. I didn't like this, but I felt confident that I could make A's by the end of the first semester.

A few days later Grandma Ellis told me that Alexander Smith's friend had stopped by to check on my grades. He had arranged for my room with Grandma as a favor for Mr. Smith. When he found that my grades were good, he left word for me to go to Williams Clothing Store and get $25.00 worth of clothes. I thought something was wrong, but I checked and was told that Mr. Smith had sent the money to be used if I was making passing grades. I bought a suit, a new shirt and a pair of shoes, which were badly needed. The first day I wore them to school they caused so much excitement and made me the center of attention, with much teasing, that I felt like a pig dressed in a pink silk dress. It was awhile before I had the nerve to wear the clothes again. Sometimes the kidding was rough, but that just made me determined to show the students that I could succeed in the classroom.

Grandma was trying to fatten me, but as I gained weight I also got taller, so I still looked like a bean pole. I began to trade some work for hand-me-down clothes from the farmers I worked for.

Harvesting was about over, but I got work helping with hog butchering and earned enough pork for Grandma to last us for most of the winter. Then I borrowed a rifle which had belonged to Grandma's husband and began to hunt. This was my speciality, and we had fresh game every day. Grandma cooked and canned part of the meat for later use. I was able to sell some rabbits. We ate like kings. We had fresh meat, canned vegetables, fresh eggs and milk, and hot biscuits or cornbread at every meal. No one ever ate better or gained less weight than I did.

When Christmas vacation came I went home to see my family and The Teacher. I had another report card, which was good, and I had done well in the classes I had never had before. I just had to see The Teacher's face when he looked at my grades.

I wouldn't spend my money on train fare, so I walked and hitchhiked. There were more cars and paved roads now, so I traveled a roundabout way so I could get more rides. I started early one morning and soon caught my first car ride. I had never ridden in a car before that. I made it halfway home the first day. Then it took me two more days to get there by walking and hitchhiking. I slept out both nights. It was really cold, but I had an old overcoat and kept a fire going all night. I would roast one side and freeze the other. I alternated sides and built up the fire every time I turned. I never decided which side was the most uncomfortable: the roasted side or the frozen side.

The next morning a farmer came by in a road wagon pulled by a team of horses. He stopped to talk and then invited me to go home with him for breakfast. I got warm while the farmer's wife cooked a big breakfast. The farmer flagged down a neighbor who gave me a ride. Many times I have thought of these good people.

Nearly ten years later I stopped at their house with my wife and two children. They didn't recognize me in the good clothes and the nice car I was driving, but they remembered the skinny, ill-dressed young man who nearly ate them out of house and home several years before. The farmer said, "We have often wondered about you." They insisted that we stay to eat with them. We kept in touch with that family through the years, exchanging Christmas cards and managing a few visits.

When I got home that night I had walked the last ten miles. My mother, like a lot of mountaineers, was embarrassed to openly show affection, but that night she hugged and kissed me every time she passed me. Father was at the lumber camp, but she told me that he had nearly quit drinking and was bringing most of his wages to her. She said that he was really proud that I was going to college and told everyone about it.

We talked far into the night as she brought me up to date on news of the family and neighbors. She said that Mr. Cramer had started night classes for adults, and she was going to learn to read and write so we could exchange letters.

Then I told her about Grandma, how she tried to fatten me up, what an interesting person she was, and how she struggled to make ends meet. I told her how we had helped each other. She gave me a room in her house, and I helped with the cow and chickens, as well as providing meat from hunting and vegetables from working on farms. Mother asked questions and wanted to hear Grandma's stories over and over, as they opened up a new world for her.

The next morning I went to see The Teacher. To me, he was The Teacher. I had good teachers at

Buford College, and I would have many more, but Mr. Cramer would always remain in my mind "The Teacher." He greeted me as if I were his pride and joy, and maybe I was. I tried to tell him everything. I had my report card for the second six weeks, and he held it in his hands all the time I was there. When he looked at me, a big smile would light up his face. He recalled the time I had butted in to argue with the textbook, and he had kept me after school to see if I knew what I was talking about.

He said, "Charles, when you told me about things the old hunter had told you when you were seven years old, and you could repeat his exact words, I knew you had the gift of a great memory. I have often wondered if it was selfish of me to take you out of your beloved woods to fulfill my dreams."

I said, "No, I am finding college as much of a challenge as hunting and trapping. The challenge of getting along with people who tease me makes it worthwhile, and I am still hunting. Besides, I would never have met Grandma Ellis, the farmers who have traded me produce for labor and have befriended me in other ways. And there's your old friend, the registrar, at Buford."

Father came home, and for the first time in our lives we talked with each other, free and easy. He gave me credit for almost cutting out his rough fighting ways, and he said he now only drank on holidays, which he named. It seemed that he still had a few more holidays per year than most people. He said, "I just told myself that I can give up the bottle except for holidays if Charles can make his way out of these mountains and go to college. I can and I will." We even teased each other about the money from pelts which I sold—money he never knew about.

Mother kept saying, "Tell him this, tell him that," until she got to hear all the stories again which I had told her the night before.

I visited old schoolmates, neighbors, brothers

and sisters. My special visits were with The Teacher, my brother Tim and my sister, Susan. Both Tim and Susan were married and had children by now.

When I got ready to go back to school, The Teacher handed me a train ticket. When I thanked him, he just said, "I am not the one to thank. Everyone helped to buy it, along with money for a few more clothes."

I had made arrangements with my friend, James McGraw, the farmer who first hired me, to have his teenage son to milk the cow and cut firewood for Grandma while I was gone. I told him I would work to repay him, but he never would let me.

Grandma really welcomed me back and used the hem of her apron to wipe her eyes while telling me how lonesome the supper hour had been while I was gone.

Extra work was slack until plowing time, so I studied and hunted more. I had to trade work for more corn, cornmeal and flour when spring plowing started.

My grades stayed almost at the top in all my classes. Time passed quickly, and soon it was time to go home for the summer. I went to see Mr. McGraw to get him to bring fruits and vegetables to Grandma during the summer, and I promised to work the debt out when I came back in September.

Again I hitchhiked most of the way home, but I made it in one day, even though I walked the last ten miles and got home late at night.

Homecoming was great fun. I couldn't wait to see The Teacher and watch him glow over my report card.

When Alexander Smith knew I was home, he came to the mountains, and we camped out and fished for trout. That was fun. That summer he got me a job with a surveying crew which was surveying land he had bought. I wouldn't let him pay me for doing what I loved to do—fishing and camping out. He didn't argue, but he said, "Go back to the clothing store at Buford. Your new clothes will be paid for."

Mr. Smith suggested that I study mathematics and learn surveying, as there was usually work in this field, and he could find a job for me. The thought scared me. I talked with The Teacher. I would have to take first-year algebra and geometry. I was good at arithmetic, but neither The Teacher nor I had ever studied those two subjects. The Teacher made a challenge out of this, saying, "You'd better try it, but your grade average will really drop." I resolved that my grades would not drop that much.

I went back to Buford again with a ticket bought by parties unknown and presented by The Teacher. My parents and I had really enjoyed each other's company that summer. Mom was the family treasurer by now, and she tried to give me some money. I wouldn't let her as I actually had more money than I had started to school with the year before. Father told me that he had cut down his drinking even more by cutting out the extra holidays he had proclaimed for himself.

Then back to Grandma. One more time she was busy using the hem of her apron to wipe her eyes "to get the dust out," she said. I came back a week early to work for Mr. McGraw to pay him for the produce he had given Grandma during the summer. They had taken the cow to the farm, milked her and brought milk and butter back to Grandma, along with vegetables to eat and can. I thought it might take all fall to work out the pay, buy they allowed me to work only two days before saying everything was paid for. The McGraws had almost adopted both Grandma and me by this time.

In the meantime I had registered for my second year of college and bought textbooks, including algebra and geometry books. I decided to study the algebra before class started. It might as well have been written in Chinese as I had no idea what was meant when I read where a + b = c. It seemed totally senseless to me and, besides, who on earth would care?

The first few days in math class everything seemed completely beyond my understanding. I understood neither the questions nor the answers. I had always had someone to help and encourage me along the way. First there was The Teacher; then Alexander Smith; then there was Grandma, the registrar and the McGraw family.

Again I got help. This time it was in my math classes, but I had never had help by anyone who looked like that girl. Several days after school started I was stopped by a girl when I was going down the hall. I could hardly believe this. I had never even exchanged a dozen words with any girl in school. I was working too much to socialize, and I was considered a little strange in speech, looks and dress to be stopped by this little beauty. She had dark hair, black sparkling eyes and a special smile.

She said, "My name is Annie James. You need help in math classes, and I had those classes in high school. I'm good in math, and I want to help you so no teacher will ever say, 'Well, Charles?' in math." With that she went tripping down the hallway. I just stood there with my mouth open. I don't think I had even answered her.

The next day she stopped me again, saying, "I will have to start tutoring you right now, or you will get too far behind." I found my voice this time and told her of my work schedule, which ended after the library closed. We finally settled for Grandma's kitchen table after the dishes were done.

Grandma agreed to this arrangement, but she put on her robe and sat with us in the kitchen in her rocking chair. She said it wasn't proper to leave a young couple alone in a room together. She would promptly go to sleep as it was after her bed time.

Annie James was serious with her tutoring, and I began to understand and even work out some of the problems. She and Grandma soon became good friends. Sometimes Annie would come before I got home, and she would help Grandma with the cooking. I guess they had a little conspiracy. Sometimes if I did real well on a problem, Annie would say, "Well, Charles," and Grandma would laugh—if she was still awake. The "Well, Charles" was still a mystery to me, and no one would tell me anything.

For the first time I began to be conscious of my appearance. If we studied a little late, it would be dark, and I would walk Annie back to her dormitory. I didn't want to embarrass her by the way I looked.

I had gained about twenty pounds in the last year, but I was an inch taller and still looked a little like a bean pole. I remembered that Mr. Smith had said that some money would be left at the clothing store for me to buy clothes. When I checked at the store I was told that $100.00 had been left for me. To me, that was a fortune for clothes. I didn't have any idea what I should buy. I asked Annie who could help me. She said, "I will. I have brothers and know what they look best in." I thought she might be embarrassed to be seen in daylight with such an odd-looking person, but she didn't seem to mind.

I told her how I had acted as a hunting and fishing guide in the mountains for Mr. Smith, and he had sent the money to the store for me to buy clothes. Then I told her about The Teacher and how he had been responsible for my coming to college.

With Annie's help and counsel, math began to be my slave instead of my master. Her advice always was, "Stay a lesson ahead of the next assignment." After awhile Annie said that I didn't need her help any more, but she would come over to see Grandma, and we could go over tough problems together.

Grandma would still laugh at Annie's "Well, Charles" remarks when I solved a problem. She laughed when Annie called her the "sleeping chaperon."

I was still puzzled why anyone would laugh when Annie said, "Well, Charles."

When six weeks tests were taken I made B's on both the algebra and geometry tests. Annie was even more pleased than I was and rushed over to tell Grandma before I came home from working. Grandma took a lot of the credit for herself, saying, "I'm the one who kept you two working, whatever that big word means that you use, which kept you working while I watched you."

Annie just answered, "You mean sleeping chaperone."

Grandma said, "I always had one eye open."

Soon I began to work problems before we got to them. I knew that I would remember them and would be called on when everyone else was stuck for the answer. Annie would sometimes pretend not to know an answer when I knew better. She liked to have me show our classmates.

One day when this happened in geometry class, the professor, with a sneaky smile, turned to me and said, "Well, Charles?" The whole class, including the professor, roared. That evening Annie told me about my nickname and why Grandma had enjoyed this little secret as much as anyone.

My parents sent a train ticket to come home for Christmas, and again The Teacher and his friends bought a return ticket. The McGraws looked after Grandma while I was gone. I still worked for the farmers for food for the table and grain for the cow. I took time out to hunt and brought in a lot of game, especially rabbits.

Annie often visited Grandma, and she and I worked on hard math problems together. By now we were both among the top students in algebra and geometry classes.

When I got my first letter from my mother, the first one she had ever written, Annie came to Grandma's house that evening and helped to figure out what Mother had written. She had been taking evening classes from The Teacher, and was learning to read and write. Grandma and Annie were almost as proud of this letter as I was. To celebrate, Grandma made a big apple pie.

I was gaining a little weight now, and Grandma took credit for that.

Mother would write often now, and her letters were getting easier to read all the time. The Teacher was doing the teaching on his own time.

The timber cutting was getting closer to home, so my Father was able to stay at home and walk to work for several months. One evening I had a letter signed by Father. I thought, "This can't be!" He had never been able to read or write. Never! I felt someone must have pulled a joke and signed his name. Soon after that I received a letter from The Teacher which cleared up the mystery. Father had been taking Mother to the night classes, even though he called it foolishness. The Teacher would tell him how well Mother was doing, saying, "I can understand where Charles gets his ability to learn. His mother is really smart." Father's competitive spirit took over. He said that anybody could learn to read and write. With challenges from The Teacher, he vowed he would show him, and he did in a fairly short time. He was a natural artist, and he had always drawn pictures for his children, so his printed letters were soon perfect. Even his first letter was very clear and readable, making it hard to believe he had written the letter. The Teacher had worked his magic again.

Summer vacation was about the same as the summer before. The McGraws took care of Grandma again. I hitchhiked home. I went trout fishing and hunting with Alexander Smith again, and he arranged for me to work with a surveying crew. I visited with my brothers and sisters. Tim and Susan were doing well. Tim had taken a correspondence course in bookkeeping and had a job in a coal company office. He had two boys now. Susan had taken some teaching courses and passed the teachers' examination and was now teaching in a one-room school. She had a boy and a girl.

I talked with The Teacher, and he was proud of my report card. He talked about how important it was for me to use my good memory, and he advised me to listen carefully to the speech and dialect of teachers from other areas. He told me that the students to Buford College had their own rural speech patterns, and since I might be working in a more urban area after graduation from college, I needed to become more aware of speech differences. It hadn't occurred to me that my fellow students weren't the ultimate in correct speech. He was always The Teacher.

In my third year I followed his advice, often practicing more correct speech when I was alone.

I gained about twenty pounds that year.

Mr. Smith again sent money for new clothes. No longer did I hear remarks about my speech, clothes and looks. In fact, Grandma said I was handsome, and Annie smiled her agreement. I also seemed to have gained a lot of respect. The only nickname I heard now was "Well, Charles," and this was mostly by the professors. This nickname was used when everyone else failed to answer a question. This was a joke to them.

That year I could have stayed in a dormitory and worked for room and board, but I could not leave Grandma, even though I had to work much harder and had no time for social life. My friend, the registrar, couldn't believe this until I explained about Grandma and what a great person she was. He seemed to understand and was really touched about my concern for her. I thought he was going to need the hem of Grandma's apron to wipe the dust out of his eyes just as she did when I went home for holidays and summer vacation, and also when I returned.

My routine remained about the same that year. During the summer The Teacher and I talked about my future plans. He was pleased that I was practicing better speech. I didn't see Annie much and missed her.

In my senior year I seemed to be one of the most respected students on campus. I was asked to accept the nomination for president of the senior class, but I had to refuse because of Grandma and necessary work. I was almost a specialist in math classes. Annie was nearly equal. She was studying to be a high school math teacher. She was elected president of the senior class. My only plans beyond graduation were that I might be a surveyor.

Annie was really popular in the social life at college, but I had little time for that. I wasn't too worried about Grandma now, for she had the McGraws, and The Teacher had prepared another student to take my place.

After Christmas vacation, the registrar and my math professor made me an appointment to meet with them. It seemed that The Teacher had been writing letters to many highly rated universities, suggesting that they consider me for a scholarship for graduate studies. Many schools had made inquiries, and a few actual offers were made. This came as a complete surprise to me. I had never given a thought to anything like this. It would have seemed too remote a possibility.

I began to think about Annie. She had been my good right arm. I had missed her a great deal last summer! I couldn't even think of life going on without Annie. I had never thought of her as my girlfriend. She was my princess, far above me—the laughed-at hillbilly. Sure, she was always there when I needed her, but that was because of her big, helping heart. She helped anyone in need.

Annie still came to see Grandma and sometimes stayed until I arrived. That evening I told Grandma, "I'm going to invite Annie over tomorrow, and I want to talk with her alone."

Grandma grunted, "I've fattened up that body of yours a lot, but I was beginning to wonder if anything was getting into your head."

I made a date with Annie the next evening at Grandma's. Annie looked at me intently and softly said, "Our first date."

Grandma left us alone in the kitchen where we had studied so much together. I told Annie about the graduate studies offers I had from various universities. Then I said, "Annie, I just can't go anywhere without you."

She didn't answer immediately. Then she came over and sat down on my lap. After putting her arm around my neck and looking into my eyes, her brown eyes sparkled as she said, "Well, just whoever told you that you were going anywhere without me?" Then she kissed me, a real princess kiss; a real princess actually kissed me.

I asked, "How could you choose me when you have your choice of any handsome boy in Buford College?"

Annie answered, "I think I am choosing the best-looking boy in college. Haven't you looked in a mirror lately? You are not the skinny hillbilly you are always talking about. You are a big man now."

"Annie," I said, "I still can't believe that you would ever consider me seriously. I thought that, to you, I was just someone who needed help. When did you begin to be serious about me?"

"Almost from the time I started helping you with math," she said. "Grandma and I often talked and agreed that in your skinny frame and underneath your odd mountain speech and clothes was a very special person. I knew then and have never changed my mind in the least."

Grandma came in from her bedroom to get a drink of water as we were catching up on a lot of missed hugs and kisses. I think she was more curious than thirsty. She had a smile on her face that stretched almost from ear to ear. When she said, "Excuse me," as she went back to bed, Annie teased her saying, "Grandma, I think you are even worse awake than you are asleep as a chaperone."

Finally I got around to telling Annie of several scholarship offers and some offers to be paid for assisting in teaching. I think we both knew she was like The Teacher and would just have to teach. Still, I spoke of the options open to us, the decisions to be made and the other problems involved.

Annie just looked at me with a mischievous smile on her face and said, "Well, Charles?"

YEARS OF SOLID GOLD

 I was nine years old when Jimmy became our neighbor after his parents bought the old Brown farm property a mile or so up the road from our place. The first time I saw Jimmy was when he came to our one-room school. He was eleven, always smiling and unusually tall for his age. He had brown hair and eyes, and he was (in my little girl's mind) the best-looking boy I had ever seen. He was polite to everyone and was always saying, "Yes, Ma'am" and "No, Ma'am" to the teacher.

Some of the boys his age thought he was a little bit sissy because of his politeness, but when they made a big issue of this they found out that he was a little bit of a tiger too.

I would sit and watch Jimmy so much that the teacher became concerned because she thought I was daydreaming. The teacher was right, except that I didn't call it dreaming. I had already decided I was going to marry Jimmy when we grew up. I didn't tell Jimmy or my classmates what I had decided, so I didn't get teased much that year.

The next year Jimmy got into a fight with Henry Jones, who was two years older and a lot bigger. Henry had Jimmy down on the ground and was hitting him. I flew into Henry, scratching, pulling hair and biting. When the fight was stopped they started teasing me about getting into the fight. I was really angry, and I said, "I'm not letting that big fat pig hurt him."

When Jimmy was teased about what I said, he was good humored and maybe pleased to be wanted, even by a baby, which boys two years older thought little girls were.

When I was teased I'd just say, "Well, I am going to marry Jimmy." I didn't even ask for Jimmy's thoughts about this.

Jimmy was in the seventh grade, and I was in the fifth grade when I realized that he would be catching the bus to high school after one more year, and it would be two more years before I could go there too, so I started studying harder to try to finish grade school early. I was able to gain that year, so I was in high school for three years with Jimmy. Everyone still teased us both about getting married.

Jimmy would laugh and say he liked being chased, although I think he really still thought girls were a nuisance, but he didn't like to hurt anyone. I would just reply, when I was teased, that was what I planned. I didn't get to see Jimmy much that year, (he went to high school before I went) because he rode the high school bus. I tried not to be pushy. I knew he was planning to go to college and would have to save money and work his way through. His parents didn't have enough money to send him, but they set aside enough of their farm to raise berries and garden produce which he could sell and save money.

I would know when he needed help to harvest the berries. My mother would let me off from work on our farm to help Jimmy sometimes, and I would go and work all day. I tried to work and not talk too much unless Jimmy wanted to tell me about his plans. Most of the time we needed to work more than talk in order to save his berries and produce. His mother would sometimes find time to help us. She seemed to like me and would sometimes tease me about my plans for Jimmy. I would just tell her that I had already picked Jimmy, and he would have to decide whether he wanted to pick me, but, if he did, I would learn as much as I could and be qualified. I would also go to college. I would have it some easier than Jimmy, for my parents could help a little more. My aunt lived in a college town and would let me have a room rent-free. I could get work as a waitress in the college cafeteria. That meant I would have a degree the same as the co-eds where Jimmy would be going. I was a little concerned about these shapely coeds, for I was tall and slender, with about as much shape as a two-by-four. I couldn't do anything about that. I could just pick more beans and berries and hope that Jimmy saw more than a skinny brat.

That year Jimmy went to college while I was a high school senior I began to fill out a little bit, but I didn't feel it was enough to compete with those girls at Jimmy's college.

We didn't see much of each other as Jimmy found a summer job. When I was asked if I was still going to marry Jimmy, I would just say, "That's my plan, but I don't know what his plans are." I would try to sound as if I was just joking, but I still meant what I told them.

We both went to different colleges that fall, and we didn't see much of each other that year as we both worked. I began to fill out and looked more like a woman. People began to tell me that I was getting prettier all the time. I was pleased and began to take better care of my appearance. Maybe now I could compete with the coeds at Jimmy's college.

The next summer Jimmy and I got jobs in stores just a block or so apart. When we saw each other for the first time Jimmy looked at me as if he was in shock, but he didn't say a word. I finally said, "We have gone to school together most of the time for nine years. You must remember me." Jimmy laughed and said, "No, I have never seen this Sharon before in my life. Are you still going to marry me?"

I smiled back and said, "That is still my plan as soon as I get you raised and break you of seeing those silly girls at your college."

He never knew that I was serious.

We saw each other a lot that summer, not dating, but having a coke together or talking for a few minutes when we would chance to meet on the street. Old friends would see us together and ask if I was still going to marry him. I would reply, "Yes, just as soon as he quits looking at those other girls at school and begins to recognize quality." Jimmy thought I was still making jokes.

The summer after graduation he came back home. He had a job as assistant professor at college while he worked to get a master's degree. One day he came to where I was working during the summer and asked to come to my house that evening so we could talk.

We sat in the porch swing after my parents had gone to bed. Jimmy sat quietly for a few minutes, and then he said, "Sharon, as long as I have known you, you always said that you were going to marry me. I have never known whether you were serious or just teasing me. Were you serious?"

I said, "I will be as honest with you as I can be. When you came to our school when I was nine years old I thought you were really cute, but what I liked about you best was your natural consideration for others. Most boys that age didn't like girls and would say so. I am sure that you didn't like them either, but you were nice about it, never saying or doing anything to hurt us, or even hurt our feelings. I knew then that I wanted to marry you, so I just said so. All during the years you never changed, even though I know you thought I was a little pest. It got to be a joke, and I went along with the joke, but, remember, I never changed my answer about meaning to marry you. I could only be helpful and not pushy. What would be, would be. Jimmy, I have never changed that goal because you have never changed."

He said, "We have never even had a date."

I responded, "But what is to stop us now?"

146

Jimmy said, "We have never even held hands."

I replied, "So let's hold hands."

He then said, "Neither have we ever hugged or kissed."

I said, "And who is stopping us now?"

No one did. I found myself in his arms where I had dreamed of being for so many years. It was a glorious feeling, even better than I ever imagined. Jimmy seemed to be in a daze. We were wrapped in each other's arms, hugging and kissing.

The porch swing, the swinging chains and the sounds of the night still echo in my memory.

At first Jimmy couldn't seem to talk, but he finally asked, "Do you want to know when I came to my senses and realized that you were the one for me?"

Of course I wanted to know.

He said it was the summer before when he had seen me for the first time in several months and realized that I was a woman and not a little girl. Mostly, though, he got to thinking about my saying that I would marry him when he came to his senses and quit seeing those silly girls. After that every time he dated one who giggled and acted silly he would remember what I had said and would start comparing all those girls with me. He went on, "All year long I kept thinking back to the times when you always appeared when I needed help the most to gather the garden produce to sell so that I could go to college. I felt guilty when I remembered that I had never really thanked you, or even appreciated how much that help was needed. I thought a lot this last school year about the little, skinny, sober-faced girl who was always at my side and ready to aid me when help was needed. Behind that face was a mischievous sense of humor. I finally knew that little sober-faced girl was solid gold."

Jimmy and I were married the following June when I finished college. I had Jim for nearly fifty-five more years. Like most young couples in those days we struggled to get started. There were many days with very little money. As time passed we prospered, and we had a family of three boys and two girls. We had many wonderful times and many sad times, as did most people. We lost one little boy.

I finally lost Jimmy after more than half a century. I remind myself that I had him all those wonderful years and to dwell on the many, many happy times. The thing that Jimmy often said to me that lifts my spirits was, "Sharon, you have always been my solid gold."

YEARS OF SOLID GOLD

I was only nine years old when I first met Jimmy
But even then, I knew he was for me
He was two years older, tall and slender
And as handsome as he could be

His eyes and his hair were the shade of brown
Like walnuts in the tree
Yes, the first time I met Jimmy Barton
I decided he would marry me

The school kids discovered my secret thoughts
One day when Jimmy got into a fight
With Henry Jones, the town bully
And I flew at Henry, swinging with all my might

When the fight was over, the kids were all laughing
At the way I'd tried to help Jim
I put my hands on my hips and stared at them all,
And said, "Some day I'm gonna marry him!"

Jimmy laughed when I said it, but he didn't act mad
He just tousled my hair as he smiled
And when the other kids teased us, he took it in stride
He never treated me like a child

With Jimmy in the seventh grade, and I just in the fifth
I knew I had to get good grades to gain
The extra time I would need to be with him in high school
I studied till I thought I was insane

We were together in high school three short years
Before college took him away
And I thought about marryin' Jimmy Barton
Without fail, every single day

When time came for him to save money for college
He'd sell produce from his parents' farm
I'd help him pick berries, and luscious ripe cherries
Sometimes he would gently pat my arm

His mama would come out and help us
Jimmy had told her about my big plan
I blushed as she gently teased me
But she said, "He'll make a good man."

He's turned a lot like his daddy
A man who will never grow old
They grow the goodness in their bones
And their hearts are solid gold

I was glad his mama liked me
It made me even more set in my mind
I knew another family like Jimmy's
Would be awfully hard to find

With Jimmy away at college
I worried a lot in my bed at night
About all those pretty college girls
And how I could keep them out of sight

He was so tall and handsome
With a head full of wavy brown curls
I was just the girl next door
How could I keep him from all those girls?

I went away to college the next summer
So I didn't see Jimmy till the spring break
And when I met him on the street
I thought, "What a wonderful husband he'll make!"

I said when he saw me, "Hello, Jimmy.
How have you been getting along?"
He stared at me with the funniest look
I thought I'd said something wrong

I said, "Hello," again softly
But he still stood there just starin'
I asked, "Don't you remember me, Jimmy?"
He replied, "I just can't believe it's you, Sharon.

You have grown up overnight before my eyes.
What happened to that skinny little kid?"
I said, "It's still me, just older you see,
And you're right—grown up's what I did!"

He laughed at me with those sparkling brown eyes
And said, "How lovely you've turned out to be
And, oh, by the way, just a bit curious
Are you still going to marry me?"

I looked him straight in those eyes
And then got up the courage to say
"That's still my plan, you're still the man
I want on my wedding day."

We spent a lot of time that summer together
Going for walks and sharing a coke
Our friends would see us and tease us a lot
They all thought my plan was a joke

The summer after my graduation, Jimmy came back home
He was working on his Master's Degree
He stopped by the five and dime where I worked
He wanted to come over later and visit with me

He dropped by after supper and we sat together
Out on the old porch swing
Things were real quiet till Jimmy finally said
"I need to discuss a few things."

All these years you been saying
You're going to marry just me
Were you making a joke
Or talking seriously?"

I thought as I answered this man that I loved
Loved him more than even my life
"Jimmy, from the first day I saw you at school
I've wanted to be your wife.

You were so thoughtful, caring and kind
You never acted like all of the rest
I haven't changed my opinion at all
I still think you're the best

"If you're here to tell me there's another
If there's someone else you want to wed
Don't worry about me, I'll be all right
And you can just forget what I've said."

Through tears, I reminded him of the words of his mama
As we sipped lemonade so frosty and cold
"Sharon, get you a man, get the best that you can
Get one that's made from solid gold."

He looked at me tenderly, with misty brown eyes
And said, "She said the same words to me
She's told me those words a hundred times."
And then he reached for me tenderly

He whispered softly, "We've never had a real date
We've never even held hands or kissed."
I took his face in my hands and said, "There's no time like
right now
To make up for all that we've missed."

When we finally stopped hugging and got back our breath
He said, "I know for sure now that you are the one
I knew it last summer when I went back to school
You were so pretty, and we had so much fun

You reminded me a lot of my mother
And the way she would act with my dad
She treated him like he was king of the world
I've always wanted a wife like my father had."

152

We married in June of the following year
And I had him for nearly fifty-five more
We had five precious children—we loved them so much
We cried together when we lost one to the Lord

As I sit on this porch swing and think of my Jimmy
Yes, he died, but he never grew old
He had the one thing that it takes to make life worth livin'
He had a heart of solid gold.

Poem by Vera Taylor

Adapted from the story Years of Solid Gold by Dennis Deitz

The following story was written in response to a cartoon drawn by a friend as a joke. The cartoon shows my wife saying that I could write a story by going out for the mail. In answer I wrote this story to drop in her mailbox.

GOING OUT FOR THE MAIL

 Even going out to the mail can be an interesting, pleasant experience. I hear the door on the mail truck slam and go out to meet the mailman. We always exchange a few little barbs in fun. If I complain about his bringing bills instead of checks, he will offer a little advice: "Why don't you use my method on bills? Go around the neighborhood and put your bills in other people's mailboxes." If I accuse him of bringing rain or snow, he always denies this, saying, "I only bring sunshine."

I accuse him of bringing bad news, saying, "It's no wonder to me that people keep dogs to bite mailmen."

He usually agrees, saying, "I'm sometimes tempted to bite myself."

Then there is the mail itself. Maybe a treasure today. There is always the millions of dollars you are about to win. The letters from Ed McMahon and *Reader's Digest* and all the copycats. The outside of the envelope saying, "You have probably won a million dollars as your name has already been placed on this special list of winners." Inside you find that there is a slight delay—you must return your special tickets by a certain magic date before becoming a millionaire. Since I have never been a millionaire before, it is not too hard to wait a few more days before I join this special group. Then I find that we have to make one of the great decisions of our lives before returning our winning tickets. We must decide whether to take five million dollars in a lump sum or by the year, totalling more than five million.

This creates one of the greatest crises in our fifty-one-year marriage. We can't agree. Not only is our marriage in jeopardy, but we are about to lose five million by not sending the winning ticket on this date. Before all is lost, we mark our choice both ways and rush to the post office, then wait to become millionaires with a broken marriage.

All of our eggs are not in one basket, though. There are still the books I wrote. The mail may bring an offer from Hollywood, from someone wanting to make a movie from one of the books. This brings a thought—"A West Virginia Hillbilly in Hollywood." I am reassured when I remember, "After all, Jed Clampett made it."

THE LOST YEARS

There I am, sitting behind a desk in an office. The man sitting across from me is apparently very angry. He is red-faced and telling me about a sub-contractor who had failed to finish a job correctly. He is blaming me because I had sub-contracted the job to him.

I had no idea who the man was or what he was talking about. I had no idea whose office I was in or why I was sitting behind the desk.

As I looked out the office window, I could see a lot of a city. Nothing looked familiar—the city, the man, the office—nothing! *I am—Who am I? What city am I in? For that matter, what state! I have to think. How can I think with this man rattling on in front of me. I have to get rid of him. I have to think.*

I managed to get rid of him with a warm smile, a firm handshake and a whole-hearted promise to thoroughly check into it in the morning. He argued his case further as I ushered him out the door. I shut the door and leaned heavily against it and took a few deep breaths to calm myself.

What am I doing here? This office seems to be mine, but the office I remember doesn't resemble this one.

I am Henry Eller! That's who I am, Henry Eller, a building contractor in Wellsville, Ohio. I have a good business and a partner. Ha! Partner, more like one of the enemy. I am also married to the enemy. She and my partner. What a pair. Surrounded, enemy on the home front, enemy in the field. Henry Eller, Wellsville, Ohio, heading for a big crash!

Well, this is not Wellsville. Wellsville is not this big. Well, if I am not in Wellsville, where am I?

The phone rang. A woman's voice said, "Mr. Thompson, I finally have Mr. Harris on the line for you."

Mr. Thompson? I thought I was Henry Eller. Who belongs to the voice on the other end? Who's this "Mr. Harris" guy?

"Thank you," I said to the voice.

"Hello, Mr. Harris. How have you been?" *Safe start.*

"I got in from Columbia and found this urgent message to call you," he said. This only added to my confusion. *Columbia, Missouri or South Carolina or wherever? My urgent call? Okay, stay safe.*

"Did you learn anything more about the matter we were discussing?" *What a stab in the dark!*

"We have discussed a lot of things lately. Which one are you asking about?" replied Mr. Harris's voice. *No help there. Wait a minute. The man who just left was complaining about an electric sub-contract. I used to be a contractor. I guess I am still in the business.*

"What about that electric contract?" I asked.

"I thought you were going to take care of that matter personally?" Mr. Harris replied with a slight edge of irritation.

"I think it has been taken care of since I made my call to you," was all I could think to say. Neither of us was of any apparent help to the other. There was an uncomfortable silence for what seemed to be minutes but was most likely closer to a few seconds. He mercifully ended it, "Henry, I'll talk to you later," and hung up abruptly.

He thinks I'm crazy. I think he's right. He did call me Henry, though it seems to be Henry Thompson instead of Eller. The engraved nameplate, which I now noticed for the first time, confirmed it.

The phone rang. "This is Judy, again. Your wife's on line two." I nearly fell out of my chair. *My wife! The wife I know is in Wellsville.* I glanced at my ring finger. There sat a plain gold band, not the gaudy one Nora insisted we buy. *Not the same ring, not the same marriage. Two wives?*

"Ah, thank you, Judy." I stammered. Line two. I stared at the phone. Luckily, only one light flashed, indicating a call on hold. I pushed the button. "Hello?"

"Hank, honey. How soon are you coming home?" I was shocked. This wasn't the high-pitched complaining voice of Nora, but a beautiful soft voice with a slight southern drawl. I sat there gasping for words and trying to think. What do you say to a wife who sounds like that! This was not the woman who would kill me if she thought she could get away with it. That thought had also crossed my mind.

I looked at my watch. It was nearly five. How long would it take to get to where I lived. Where did I live? And with whom? Were there children? I rubbed my forehead. I was getting one heck of a headache. *I've got to give myself some time.*

"Ah, it won't be much longer. I'll leave by five thirty." I replied.

"Will you pick up some bread and milk on the way home? Dinner is almost ready and the children are already watching for you," said the beautiful voice.

"Okay," I said and hung up. A new wife and more than one child for the voice had said "children." How many and how old? I needed time to think but I had only a half an hour to figure out who to go home to, where "home" was and how to get there.

The door opened and a young woman walked in. "I'm leaving now, Mr. Thompson. Do you need anything before I go?" Did I ever. Her voice matched the one of the phone so this must be Judy, my secretary. Maybe she could give me some answers. I made general conversation about the "family" hoping that she would fit a name in here or there to no avail. Judy left.

Where could I find information about myself? I pulled out my billfold and pulled out my driver's license. There I found my name and address, and a surprise. The picture on the license was a man who looked like I would have looked if I were about ten or so years older, gray around the temples. I read the rest of the license. Height and weight were O.K. Date of birth was right. Date of issue. *That can't be right. It's only*—The desk calendar proved it. *I've lost twelve years! This is me? I'm . . . forty-two years old!* A mirror. I went out in the hall. There was a water fountain just down to the left and luckily restrooms across the hall. The mirror of the men's room showed an exact likeness of the drivers photo. *Where have I been for the last twelve years?*

Another look in my billfold produced a business card. It read "Henry Thompson, Building Contractor." I went to the phone book in my office. The address listed for Henry Thompson matched the one on my driver's license. *Now, to find my house.* I rifled through my desk trying to find a city map to no avail. I stared at the wall for inspiration. There, on the wall across from me was a map stuck with colored pins, "Newburg, South Carolina" was written across the bottom. Summit Avenue ran past the office and within a few blocks of my house.

I grabbed the car keys out of my pocket and froze. *I can't remember what kind of car I've got. Where is my car? There's no registration card in my billfold. I'll just have to hunt for it.* Luckily, outside next to the office building was a small parking lot. I found a car that fit the keys in a space marked "Reserved" and a registration card in the glovebox.

O. K., milk and bread. I drove down Summit Avenue and spotted a Get 'N Git convenience store. "Come again, Mr. Thompson," the check-out girl said.

Only five blocks to go. I hope the numbers are on the house or mailbox. Won't look good for me to be wandering up and down my own street. "Henry Thompson 223 Palmetta Street" showed on the mailbox as I pulled up and parked in the drive. Going towards the front door, I took a deep breath, reached for the doorknob and walked in.

Walking towards me was one of the most beautiful women I had ever seen, with a big smile on her face. She walked into my arms, hugged me close and tight, and gave me a long kiss. This intimacy from a gorgeous woman whom I didn't remember ever seeing almost sent me into orbit. A little girl of about six and a boy maybe two years older were hugging me too. *What a beautiful family—my family. And I can't even remember ever having seen them before or any of their names.*

"Dinner is nearly ready," the beautiful stranger said with a smile.

Where is the bathroom? I need to wash up. I can't just ask. My daughter came to my rescue by asking, "Tell me a story about one of your trips to outer space." *Don't know what I've already told her but this sure is an opening.*

"I'm from the moon. You know, the Man on the Moon? We don't have houses like this. Can you show me around?"

She loved it, being tour guide to an alien. "This is my room. This is David's room, and the bathroom. Here's Mommy and Daddy's room." The words "Mommy and Daddy's room" struck me like a blow. I was to sleep with this beautiful stranger. To me that would be like desecrating a goddess. I was maybe a bigamist or even worse. How could I sleep with this beautiful woman—innocent of my background? *Boy, I'm being a prude. I don't remember being one before, so why do I feel this way now?* But my daughter was continuing her litany, ". . . my daddy's office." I put my briefcase down inside the door of the office. *Hope its contents can help*

160

solve the mystery of the last twelve years.

Dinner went fairly well. The children wanted me to tell more about the stories I seemed to have been making up for them. I brushed them aside since I had no idea what they were. I would just make up new ones instead.

After dinner was over and the children in bed, my wife and I talked. She never gave me any clues about us, our past or my business. A battle took place within me between my desire to share a bed with her and my determination not to. My determination won out. I told my beautiful wife I had business I needed to attend to in my office. She seemed to be used to me working late at home.

Several hours later, I remembered my past well but not one thing about the past twelve years. The last thing I remember as "Henry Eller" was sitting in front of a motel near Dayton, Ohio. I had $75,000 cash in my pocket, money from the construction company. My partner and wife handled the books and money. I had written the $75,000 check from a bank in another town where we were working on a large construction job and needed a lot of money in the local bank for supplies and wages. I planned to open a personal account in case they had taken all the money from the business.

Everything was blank from that point on. I had no idea what had happened. Had I murdered both of them? Nora was a nightmare in my life. I would have helped her pack to go with my partner if they hadn't been dipping in the till. Or, had I just walked out myself? How was I going to find out?

What about the money I had? If I had put it in the bank, I thought I would later prove that I had put it there for safekeeping. I must have kept it in cash. *Does this mean that my wife and ex-partner could prove embezzlement? If so, I'm in deep trouble.*

I have to find out. And I have to find out before I tell my new wife. Ellen, I had found, was her name.

We may not even be legally married. I've got to know the past before I can confide in her. I'm a murderer, a thief or both. I've got to leave. I can't find out anything here.

I started going through all the papers I could find in the office, both business and personal. First, about the contracting business. Would it fold or go broke without me? How could it run with me? I didn't remember anything about any of our jobs. I just had to hope that my secretary, new partner and any foreman on the job could run things for awhile.

The business was sound. It had a good cash flow and I found records of stock and bond certificates. Our personal finances were also sufficient enough that my family could live comfortably for a year without me and still have expense money for me to solve my mystery.

Ellen opened the office door and came in. What a lovely lady! "Hank, I couldn't sleep. I had a strange feeling that something was wrong. Is anything bothering you? Can I help?"

I looked into her eyes for a long time, studying the beautiful woman who was a stranger to me. Finally, I answered, "You are the only one that can. Would you trust me even if I can't tell you anything for awhile?"

"Haven't I trusted you for ten years without knowing anything about you?" she answered.

"I don't know. When I walked into this house a few hours ago, so far as I know I had never seen you or the children before in my life." A lovely family that I don't even know was all I could think.

"No, no, no, it can't be," she said between sobs. She was sitting on my lap with her head on my shoulder. I was crying too.

"I have to leave to find out what may have happened after my memory left me back north. It could be real bad. So bad that you will never want to see me again. It may be nothing more than a bad knock on the head, but I have to know. I don't know how long it will take."

I questioned Ellen about our past. It was strange calling this woman by her first name considering I had only known her or at least remembered her a few hours before.

We had met, she said, at a friend's house nearly twelve years before and soon fell in love. She had wondered about my past, which I never talked about, evading all questions. She said, "I quit asking and just started believing in you and not worrying about your past. I never once believed that you had done anything bad."

"I have never done anything bad that I remember but I don't know what happened after I blacked out and I'm worried about that. I just have to know."

Ellen knew a lot about my business and assured me that the employees were capable of carrying out all present signed contracts but that no one could continue with new contracts. She said our personal finances were much higher than I had surmised. She could handle our affairs.

She agreed to tell everyone that a family emergency had come up and I had to go home for awhile. By this time, it was daybreak Saturday, a good time to leave, giving her time to tell everyone I had left on an emergency trip.

We just clung to each other until the children got out of bed. Ellen helped me pack. The children were told that Daddy had to leave on a trip.

I finally tore myself away from the three of them—this beautiful family I had known for eighteen hours, got in one of our cars and headed north. North to Ohio—to what, I had no idea—to jail for all I knew.

I drove north, my mind in a turmoil, hating to leave my new (to me) family. I wanted to stay and really get acquainted and enjoy them. There was Ellen, the beautiful soft-spoken one who is supposed to be my wife, but is she? Is she really my legal wife? All I knew of her was what I had learned in less than twenty-four hours. I can't bear the thought of doing further wrong by being with her until I know about my past. How could I have married her, not remembering anything? Have I been married before? What kind of a person am I? Had I ever been in love, like I was with Ellen?

Certainly not with Nora. That was more of a "why not get married" marriage. Nora had come to work for me soon after I came to Wellsville and began my own construction company. She was hired to keep books and do secretarial work. She was efficient and pleasant. When business boomed, Nora became all sweetness. I found myself married to a girl who seemed to have already spent all of her sweetness on me. Then I became acquainted with Dan Douglas, a businessman who seemed to have several deals going, including construction work. Somehow we became partners. Dan was married, had some money, business connections, lots of promises and some money to invest. Nora seemed to have been the one who convinced me that Dan had a great reputation as a businessman. In any case, I ended up with a wife and a business partner, both eager to share any of my business successes with me.

Dan never lived up to his built-up reputation, but did give some help. He seemed to stay around the office helping Nora with office work more than anything else. Nora became harder and harder to live with and work with after our marriage. I needed to work out of town a lot on construction jobs. I just stayed out more than was necessary, to avoid controversy.

I became concerned about money and the book-keeping when I was about to sign a contract to build a large apartment complex. I had to know our cash flow—how much money we had available, etc. When I started checking the books, bank accounts

and assets, Nora was very upset and even belliger-
ent. When I tried to explain that I had to know
before I signed the contract, she almost refused to
let me see the records. Dan backed her up in this.
They claimed that I was insulting them. This was
proof that something was wrong. This was when I
cashed a $75,000 check from a finished contract,
planning to put it in a personal account, to offset
money they must have drained from the company.
If Dan and Nora had this business relationship,
they probably had a personal relationship, so I
started trying to prove the latter. What had happened after I caught them at the motel room, I had
no idea. I had just blacked out. I knew that I was
very angry. I was far more angry that the business
was going broke than because of a relationship
between them. They deserved each other, but had I
killed them? I didn't know. My memory was gone.

The big problem facing me now was how to find
out without being arrested for, maybe, murder,
embezzlement or bigamy. I think that bigamy concerned me as much as the more serious charges.
Then I would lose Ellen and and the children. I just
couldn't stand the thought.

Now I was in northern Kentucky, nearing Ohio.
I had no plan, nor yet any good ideas. I still had an
hour or two before I found a motel and made my
plans to solve my problem.

I arrived and got a motel near Dayton, Ohio,
about fifty miles from Wellsville. I sat and made
plans. I first went over the names of people I had
known in Wellsville and the surrounding towns
where I had worked and built buildings. I had
made a lot of acquaintances, but due to a lot of
travel I had few really close friends. I came up with
no one I felt I could really trust in case I had committed a serious crime. It wouldn't be right to
involve anyone else.

I worked out a starting plan. I didn't shave and
started growing a beard, feeling that I wouldn't be

easily recognized. Twelve years had made a difference. My hair was partially gray and it looked as though my beard might be almost white.

The next day I went to a Dayton newspaper office to check old newspaper files. If murder had been committed, I would surely find it in the files. I remembered the date I had disappeared and checked files for seven days after the date of my memory loss. I found a lot of items with a Wellsville dateline, but nothing of concern to me. No murders, no charges of embezzlement or disappearance.

I felt a lot better until I thought about amnesia. I knew very little about it. Maybe I had continued with this earlier life and could remember then but not now. I had no idea. Maybe I would have to check newspaper files for weeks or months.

Then I thought of my earlier life and boyhood. I thought of my mother, father and brother, George. How could I have just now thought of them? We had been a very close family living in a small town in Pennsylvania near Scranton. My father, too, had been a contractor, building mostly houses in steel and coal towns. We were never rich, but Father always made a good living, sending both boys to college. I had worked with him through high school and college and learned the building business. That, along with college, is where I learned the construction business. My brother, George, became a chemical engineer and had gone to work for a chemical company. He was never interested in building things as I was.

I ran to the telephone to get the telephone number of my parents. There was no telephone listed under the name of Henry Eller, Sr. I was devastated. Then I remembered that my father had retired and planned to move south. Where, I had no idea as he hadn't decided the last I knew. My parents would now be about sixty-five years old. They might even be dead for all I knew.

Could I find my brother? The last I knew he had changed jobs a couple of times, getting better jobs each time.

It would be hard to find them. Besides, I didn't really want to, until I found out whether I was in trouble or not. Still, I sure wanted to know whether they were living.

My beard was longer now and white. I felt I could go back to Wellsville and not be recognized if I stayed away from public places. When I drove through Wellsville, very little had changed. I drove by my old construction buildings. The company was still in operation. The sign read "Wellsville Construction Company" and the company seemed to be doing well. The buildings were well kept with a lot of trucks and new machinery around them.

Who was running it? Was it my ex-wife and ex-partner? This would be surprising as Dan had proved to be lazy and not very knowledgeable. Had Dan divorced and then married Nora? In a town this size, their affair would surely be known. Had they brought charges against me for embezzlement?

I just stopped, walked into an office. When I opened the door, I planned to walk back out if I saw a familiar face before they had a chance to see me. The receptionist was a young girl. I just told her that I needed to call the owners for an appointment. I was lucky that she just gave me some business cards showing who to call for the various people who handled various phases of the business. The cards included the names of the president and vice president. One name was James Hayes. I had known a James Hayes in the construction business who was from Dayton. Maybe it was the same person. This seemed likely. I sure didn't want to meet him as he might know me.

I started back toward Dayton with no plans for the moment. I passed a large truck. On the side of the door read "Wellsville Construction Company."

167

This gave me an idea. I let him pass me, then followed some distance behind. He stopped at a restaurant as I had hoped, then I followed him inside. He was a young man so he wasn't apt to know me.

He sat on a stool at the lunch counter. There was an empty stool beside him, so I took it. After we ordered, he struck up a conversation with me as I had hoped. Also, he was a talker and I was a great listener. He wasn't a lot of help until he started talking about the owners. He said that James Hayes was from Dayton and still had a company in Dayton.

The truck driver kept talking. I was able to guide the conversation a little by an occasional question. I hoped I sound a little uninterested. I asked if the owners had started the business. He said that he had been with the company for only four years, but had heard that they had bought it. He went on to tell that there was gossip about the former owner. He said that he was told that two partners and a wife to one of them just disappeared, all about the same time, almost leaving the business in limbo.

There still seemed to be a lot of speculation as to what had happened to the three of them. Some people speculated that the husband had killed his wife and partner. Some believed it might have been the other way. A lot of money seemed to have disappeared at the same time.

There was an investigation. Officials didn't know what charges to bring. There were no bodies, no evidence of foul play. What charges could be brought for persons stealing their own money, while leaving assets, until one of them brought charges?

This was interesting and I was elated until I gave all this further thought. I first had in my mind to go the law officials and tell them who I was and help them solve the case. Suddenly it occurred to me that this was putting my head in a noose. I would be furnishing a prime suspect for murder—me.

I decided to try going to the courthouse which was about fifteen miles from Wellsville. I had never gone there very often. Dan usually took care of this part of our business. With my short beard I felt that I shouldn't be recognized even by someone I had once known. Yet, I didn't want to look at criminal records, as this might draw too much attention to me.

I mostly browsed through records that were more open records. I watched for the name Henry Eller. Of course, it appeared often because of business and land records, but not in the other few records that I checked.

I looked at divorce records. There was a record of Amy Douglas suing Dan Douglas for divorce. The date was two weeks after the time I must have disappeared. The name of the correspondent was Nora Eller, whose maiden name had been Nora Smith. This was strange. I had married Nora Heffner. I always thought that this was her maiden name. Then who was Heffner? Nora had never mentioned anyone named Heffner or having been married. I could find no record of divorce hearings or alimony or settlement. I presumed that it might be in other records. If it wasn't, then what did this mean? I now thought it might be possible that Dan and Nora had stayed until all contracts had been paid, took everything they could in cash, then disappeared. This would also avoid a divorce settlement. All of this was only a guess on my part. How could I prove anything? I thought of Dan's divorced wife.

I checked the telephone book and found a listing for her. She could help if I dared to talk to her, but she might recognize my voice, although I had never talked to her very much.

After going back to the motel, I went over everything in my mind in order to make further plans. Everything I came up with was negative. I didn't dare check records. I couldn't talk to anyone I had known before. I couldn't talk to Dan's wife. I couldn't hire detectives. Everything might lead back to me and maybe I had killed them.

I finally reached the conclusion that I had to take a few chances. I just had to talk to people and look up records.

I decided to start with Dan's wife. I had to make up a good story to tell her and hope she could help me.

I made the call and Mrs. Douglas answered. Apparently my voice wasn't familiar to her. I told her that I was a private investigator and been hired to find the owners of our old construction company. I made up a story of how the owners had bought almost worthless swampland. It was now filled and was about to be valuable. Their signatures were needed if they wanted to sell. I had been hired to find the owners.

Mrs. Douglas was bitter and talkative. Her husband and Nora just disappeared at the time. His partner (me) was also gone, but she didn't know whether it was at the same time or earlier. All cash had disappeared at the same time, leaving the business in a mess.

Everyone made claims against the business, including the Internal Revenue Department. Of course, she wanted to know about the valuable land I had made up. I could plead ignorance, saying that I hadn't been told much, but was hired to find the owners. She said detectives had been hired to find Dan and Nora with no luck.

I asked about Dan and Nora's families. They were both from the area. Both had families still in the area, but members swore that they knew nothing about Nora and Dan after they left. She kept talking.

One thing was of special interest to me. Nora's

family living in the area were Smiths. Nora's name had been Smith. She had married John Heffner, who had left her, accusing her of having an affair with Dan Douglas. Then Nora had married me. Dan became my partner. There was talk that Nora was never divorced from John Heffner. This would be great news if I could prove it. I wouldn't be a bigamist. Ellen and the children would be mine legally.

When I finally hung up, I wasn't sure whether the information, although helpful, was worth the chance I had taken. I was sure that this non-stop talking woman would discuss the conversation with everyone, including the authorities. It might cause the case to be reopened.

I now believed that I wasn't the No. 1 suspect in the case originally. I believed that Dan and Nora were. If I reappeared, I would become the No. 1 suspect.

At first I was a little worried about telling Mrs. Douglas about this mythical land that had become valuable. She would probably tell a lot of people about it. As I thought more about it, I decided to play this angle up a little more. Maybe something would come from it. I called my old construction company and talked to an assistant manager.

I told him that I represented a corporation which was interested in purchasing some land that had once been bought by their predecessors. I needed to find the old owners or know who now owned the land and if it was for sale. He questioned me and I made up quite a story, hinting that this once worthless land might be valuable.

I went to nearby Fairfield, Ohio and rented a box at the post office. From there I went to the local newspaper and ran an ad asking for the whereabouts of the former owners of the Douglas and Eller Construction Company of Wellsville or anyone with authority to sign a deed for some land once belonging to them. Any answers were to be sent to the post office number.

I didn't plan to open the box. I thought that it might be watched. I was just interested in seeing what might happen. Maybe Dan or Nora would reappear to claim the money for the land. They might now feel that the only danger they faced was for alimony for Dan's ex-wife.

I really didn't have any definite idea about what I could accomplish by this except to stir things up, maybe even putting me into danger again. I was anxious to find something out—almost anything. I wanted to get on with my life with the beautiful Ellen and the children. I was real anxious to know about my parents and my brother, George. Yet, I wasn't anxious to know my old family then crush them because of my troubles.

I spent my extra time in libraries. I wanted to know more about finding missing persons. It was up to me to find them. I didn't feel safe enough to hire detectives, as this might expose me.

I called Ellen about once every week. She assured me that the business was still going O.K. with my old contracts. New business was at a standstill. She was now working at the office, looking after our interests and making excuses about my absence. She was a sweetheart about questioning me, knowing that I had problems on my mind. She seemed to take it as our problems, not just my problems. I still couldn't bring myself to tell her more. I was afraid I would lose her.

During our conversation she volunteered that she had often wondered about my earlier life, but didn't ask, feeling that I was to be trusted. Then she said, "Nothing in our ten years together changed my mind."

I said, "Ellen, I still don't know whether your trust was right or wrong. I am still trying to find out." Then I asked her a key question. "When you first knew me, did I have a lot of money?"

Ellen told me that when she met me I had a

nice construction business, but she guessed that I must have had money or had made a lot of money quickly.

I still couldn't bring myself to tell her more. I continued going to the library, reading books on amnesia, books on searching for missing persons and even true stories about finding missing people. This was interesting and gave me a lot of ideas, but I had no place to start.

One day at the library, I picked up some chemical magazines. I was leafing through one of them and here suddenly was a picture of my brother, George, looking back at me. I dropped the magazine, totally amazed.

The magazine told me everything. The chemical company he worked for, the city where he was living and his high position with the company as he had just received a promotion.

I had made up my mind to not contact any of them until my problems were solved. I supposed that they had given me up for dead. The shock of finding me and knowing the troubles I might now be in could well be too much.

I didn't know what to do. I wanted desperately to know about my parents. I didn't want them to know about me. Not yet, until my problems were solved.

I decided to go back to the motel room and just think, then decide. I settled in my room and went over my earlier life carefully in my mind.

Mostly I tried to remember more about George, our relationship and the kind of person he was. I remembered that as boys we had been real close. We had a close relationship with our parents. All of us had gone on vacations together, camped together and played games together.

We had grown a little apart when I went to college. I had loved working with our father and loved the construction business. George hadn't liked this work and studied chemical engineering in college.

Neither Father nor me understood this and sometimes told him so. There was no major problem because of this, but we just grew apart a little more. Later, I began to realize that George, being the younger brother, might just want to be his own man.

I finally made my decision. I was going to call George. This was not as easy as I thought. Information did not have a listing in the city where he worked, as he happened to be living in a town close to there. I wanted to talk to him when he was at home, not in his office. I finally called the chemical company and got a receptionist. She couldn't give out his home number. I told her that I was an old friend from his hometown. I needed to talk to him privately. She then called him and asked him to call my motel number at 8 p.m. that evening. I guessed that he only agreed to this out of curiosity as I only told her to have him call "John."

I didn't think that he would even call and I would maybe have to travel to Michigan. I went back to the motel room and waited and waited. It was only 6 p.m. when I started waiting. That two hours was forever.

At exactly 8 o'clock the telephone rang. The voice sounded impatient, saying, "This is George Eller. You wanted me to call."

I just asked, "Are you alone and sitting down?"

He replied, "Yes. What difference does it make?"

I told him, "Because you might be shocked. This is your brother, Henry."

He almost screamed, "Henry, where in Hades have you been? Mom, Dad and me have never missed a day worrying about you."

I asked, "How are they? Are they living?"

He said, "Yes," but he was upset that I hadn't called them, insisting that I call them right now. He insisted that I take their telephone number and call them in Florida.

I said, "George, I can't. You have got to listen to

me first. I may be in deep trouble. You will then understand."

George just stopped and listened while I told my story. "George, the last twelve years have been a total blank. One week ago I had no memory of you or of my parents. One day at my desk I knew everything before twelve years ago and nothing about the last twelve years."

"Now I may be in deep trouble. I just don't know what happened before my mind went blank. It is possible that I committed a serious crime. I'm here to find out. I can't call Mom and Dad until I know."

He was silent for awhile, then said, "Drive on up to Michigan, get a motel room and call me where we won't have company to disturb us. I may know some things that will help."

I waited until the next morning and drove to Michigan. That evening I called and we met. Even with all my troubles this meeting was a great reunion. This was the brother of my boyhood. We felt close again, regretting the years apart from each other. He understood why I didn't want to call my parents yet.

Then George told me what he knew about my disappearance. It was a little while before they knew I had actually disappeared. They were not able to get me on the telephone. At first they could get Nora by telephone and she would just say I was out of town on a job. Later, they couldn't even get Nora.

Our parents were frantic. George came to Wellsville, investigated and hired a detective. By this time my ex-partner and ex-wife had disappeared, according to rumor. Before they left, Dan and Nora had spread a rumor that I had left with the money. Both of their families had a lot of influence and were able to keep any rumors from newspapers.

After Dan and Nora disappeared, the law officers found that a lot of the checks were cashed after my disappearance. This shifted the suspicion back to Dan and Nora, in the opinion of the officers, and caused them to look harder for Dan and Nora than for me.

This was encouraging, but if I suddenly reappeared, the suspicion would shift back to me. George was totally fascinated with my story of my waking or whatever, and finding a family that I didn't know about. He was also concerned that Ellen might never forgive me if I had married her when I already had a wife.

As it happened, George's wife was at her parents' house for a few days caring for her mother. Their son and daughter were away at college. He didn't have to explain why he was out at night.

We both felt that it was better that we not meet at his house. Friends and neighbors might wonder about me if they dropped by. There was no doubting that we were brothers. We could talk and plan in my room without any interruptions from the telephone.

We discussed every phase of my problem and how to solve it. We both had ideas and rejected them. We had some ideas that we might pursue later. I mentioned to George that I had planted this little story about the corporation or one of us partners having land that had become valuable. George was real intrigued with that and wanted to discuss this to see what other ideas we might come up with.

George remembered that after my disappearance, he and our parents had hired a private detective agency to look for me. He still had the old reports. We weren't sure whether it was wise to contact them and arouse suspicions again. George kept mentioning the idea I had planted about the valuable land. He thought somehow this idea could be pursued. We came up with no concrete ideas. So, I would just go back to Dayton and do some more looking and listening.

The meeting with George was such an up-lift. The reunion was great and the news of our parents was so good. I still had troubles but the fact that I now had someone to help on my side was a real boost to my morale.

After returning to Dayton, I made my first trip to the P. O. box I had rented. I wasn't about to open the box, but I could see through the glass front without getting near it. A man stood in the lobby. I wondered if he might be watching my P. O. Box. I went to the window, bought stamps, taking my time. The man was still busy with papers in the lobby. My ad had at least stirred up some activity. There were several letters in my P. O. Box. I would have loved to see them but didn't dare. It was always possible that the man in the lobby was a policeman. Maybe it was one of Nora or Dan's relatives smelling some money. Maybe it was a friend of Dan's ex-wife who was still looking for alimony. I was determined not to go near that box.

By now, I had found the favorite catting places for the truck drivers from my old construction company and when they usually stopped by. I would sometimes be there with my briefcase to go with my new identity as a salesman. I would only strike up conversations with the younger drivers; the older men might have recognized me. I didn't have to ask many questions. I overheard enough to know that my ad was causing a lot of talk. If any of Nora's or Dan's relatives had heard about the valuable land, they would let them know. Though it was possible that neither of them were still in touch with their families.

I would call and talk to Ellen and the children every few days. I still couldn't go back. Until I knew more about whether I was a bigamist, I felt guilty about resuming a married relationship with Ellen. It didn't seem fair to this beautiful stranger who was my wife.

She was so easy to talk to. I couldn't believe

how understanding she was. She never asked "Why, why, why." I couldn't explain. It would just get too complicated. How this lady could accept things in blind trust, I didn't know. It was not that easy with the children. They just wanted me to come home.

When I went back to Michigan, George's wife had returned. So, we still thought it best to meet in the motel. He had told too many friends about his missing brother. If they ever saw us together, they would know who I was. George explained to his wife that the meetings concerned me and finding me. We weren't ready to let anyone know that I was around.

When we met to go over our strategy and make plans, we both had new ideas. George had contacted the detective agency in Dayton. They were still in business. The man who had worked on my case was a partner in the agency now. George only told them that he would be in contact later. We decided to hire them. We wanted to look for Dan and Nora, but still thought the best method would be to spread the land story. But we didn't trust them enough to tell them it was a false story.

We decided to convince Nora and Dan that the story was true. This wouldn't be that hard. I had often taken options on land which might be used in the future to build on. If I could not build on the land, a customer might buy it. Sometimes, I might buy and then sell it for profit. Sometimes, I bought an option or land under another name, keeping our contracting name out of it, to keep the prices of the surrounding property down. It would be logical that Dan and Nora would believe I may have done this and even that the land might be in our old company name.

The problem with the story was explaining why the land had not become delinquent or who had paid the taxes. We decided that it could have been done in some way so that we didn't have to prove

anything since greedy people want to believe anything which might bring them money.

George hired the detective to look for the land
titles, deeds, tax receipts, etc. for the land. The
purpose was to spread the rumor and maybe bring
Dan and Nora out into the open.

In Dayton, I would stop by the post office once
in a while to mail letters. There seemed to be someone in the lobby each time. I would never even
glance at the rented box. I was fairly sure that it
was being watched.

There seemed to be a lot of interest created by
the rumor. There were even a few short articles in
newspapers, especially small town newspapers.
The items in the papers had little information but
mostly speculation as to where this land might be
and who held the deed and in what name. They
hadn't found a connection with our old construction
company or any of the owners. They did have the
story of the P. O. box number and the assumed
name I had used to rent the box.

From what I read it seemed that the local
authorities were not yet involved, but people love a
mystery. Maybe Dan's ex-wife had told her story of
the strange telephone call. No one seemed to take
her seriously as she had been telling stories for
almost ten years.

Then the stories began to change. They had
made the connection between the construction company and the valuable land. By this time, people
were coming from everywhere with tales of close
relatives, some deceased, who they were sure had
made investments in assumed names, bringing
with them all kinds of proof.

Then came a call from George. It was a real
bombshell. It seems that the detective agency had
run ads in little county weekly papers in southwest
Ohio. That was why the sudden increase in "would-
be owners." Why hadn't I thought of it? That was
an air raid warning. The bomb was that they had

found the land! George was skeptical saying, "How could he find it since we made up the story about the non-existent land?" How indeed? I had no idea what he had found. I told George to get all the information he could from the detective agency and that I was on my way.

On the drive north, I became more and more concerned about the odd coincidence. Was it possible that Dan and Nora might have taken money from the firm and invested it?

When George came to my motel room, he had all the details. The detective had run the ad in a small weekly about 150 miles east of Wellsburg. A real estate man answered stating that he held a deed, not recorded, in a safety deposit box. He had power of attorney to rent, lease and sell timber or mineral rights for 500 acres of land. He was also paying taxes from the income. The agreement and deed were made out to a Henry Eller. George had the name of the real estate man. The strangest piece of information was that the man said that this nearly worthless piece of land had just become very valuable. It was exactly like the story we had circulated. The real estate man told the detective that he had been told to only contact me and no one else in the construction company. When he found out that the construction company had been sold, and that I had been gone for several years, he had been trying to find me, quietly. He was happy to find someone to give him authority to make a big sale.

Slowly it came back to me. Not long after Nora and I had taken Dan in. as a partner, I began to realize that there were problems between us. I had money in my personal account in Wellsburg. In addition, I had a savings account in a bank in Dayton. It was a reserve account, not needed by me or the company. For some reason, I just never told Nora about this account. I had a feeling that I shouldn't. After we were married, Nora began to question me about everything, including personal money, causing me to ask the bank not to send statements; I would just pick them up at the bank.

About this time, a small manufacturing company contacted me to find some land and give them a price to build a factory. I had worked with this company before near Wellsburg. This time, they wanted to build south of Columbus, far enough out so that land prices would be lower. I contacted a young real estate agent who was starting his own business. We never found what the company needed, mostly due to high voltage line. The agent showed me a piece of property as a possible site. It was almost worthless as farm land. Most of it was swampy bottomland with high ridges between, too steep to farm. It didn't fit the needs of my potential builder but the agent, a real go-getter, mentioned the possibilities of this land as a long-term investment. He pointed out that the sale price was low because the many heirs wanted to sell and divide the money. With a price that low, it could always be sold for more than the investment price.

The property already had a little store and a service station leased. Plus a few acres leased to farmers as well as some timber. He also said that the rumors were that a four-lane highway might be built through this area someday. I could see that the ridges could be bulldozed into the swamp lands after they were drained, making a very valuable piece of property.

I wasn't too excited about the prospects, but this could be a place to invest the savings that Nora wouldn't know about. I worked out a deal with the agent. The deed was made out. The agent would keep it in a safety deposit box and I would get a copy. I gave him power of attorney to collect rentals, which were small but enough to pay the low taxes. I told him to never write and to contact only me. I would be in touch. This pretty well wiped out my savings account.

Though some of my earlier memories had returned, this part did not return until the detective found the land. I'm not sure that George fully believed me but only kept saying, "How was it possible that you thought up this story?"

I had no idea unless it was a subconscious memory. I said, "George, you also helped to concoct this story."

If Dan and Nora were alive, this might bring them into the open. On the other hand, old problems remained. George could now appear openly as a brother trying to settle an estate. I couldn't appear until Nora and Dan appeared. I might be charged with murder. I couldn't appear until I could prove that they were alive. Neither could they appear until I appeared. They might be charged with my murder. We were at a standstill.

The part that concerned me as much as anything was proof that I was not a bigamist. My new family and having Ellen as my legal wife was all-important to me. I just couldn't go back home until I had this proof. It was almost an obsession with me. I felt that if I went back as a husband, that would be unforgivable, now that I had doubts about whether I was her legal husband. I nearly died wanting to see them. I would call and they would beg me to visit. This part was pure agony. I had no logical excuses.

George and I did decide to have the detective go ahead and spread the word about where the valuable land lay and even build up the story of value. We hoped that Dan and Nora's people would make claims and maybe leave clues as to where they now were.

The first claim that we heard was from James Heffner, Nora's ex-husband. He didn't get a lawyer. He just appeared at Wellsville, saying that he was entitled to a part of the value as Nora's husband. Of course, I had never known of him as I thought Heffner was Nora's maiden name. He told that they were married at seventeen, soon separated, but that Nora had never divorced him. He now worked as a laborer and lived about fifty miles from Wellsville. Our detective found that this man was totally uneducated. He had no idea that if Nora had no divorce from him that she would not be legally married to me and therefore, she couldn't legally inherit anything from me. I was glad that he hadn't consulted a lawyer.

George had the detective look for the divorce papers. If we could prove that they were never divorced, then my marriage to Ellen was legal. I just hoped that Ellen would accept this and forgive me. Yet, how could a negative like this be proved?

At least, the land I owned would give me something to keep me busy, By now, I remembered all about it and where to find it.

I drove east and got a motel room at Jackson, Ohio. The land was about fifty miles away. I could have stayed nearer, but didn't want to run into my real estate man, as he might recognize me, although I could claim to be my brother, George. The real estate man had only known me for a few days, years ago, but why take a chance?

The next morning I went to see the land. I was surprised that I remembered where the boundary lines were. I had looked at the land pretty thoroughly for possibilities for the interested manufacturing company. I hadn't been interested personally until later. It hadn't changed much. A few more little businesses had appeared around the edges and some patches of timber had been cut. The new four-lane highway, running from Cincinnati to Athens, Ohio, called the Appalachian Highway, was being graded.

I remembered surveying the land in my mind. The ridges could be graded off into the swamp, leaving a solid base for building. The new highway was in sight of the land, with a convenient exit planned. This was interesting and took my mind off of other troubles, at least for a day or two. It was also refreshing to me as a contractor to think of all the possibilities here.

I gave little thought to becoming rich. Too many other problems had to be solved first. Maybe I would never receive a penny from the land. If Nora and Dan reappeared, they might even get the money. This would be the one thing I would fight all the way.

There was also the possibility that Nora and Dan had robbed our company before leaving and that a huge debt had been left. Maybe they had not paid the last year's income tax or withholding taxes. If so, the added penalties and interest might be far more that this land was worth. Would I still be responsible for that since the construction company had been a partnership? It was possible.

The detective was now doing all of the footwork. I didn't have a lot to do, so time passed slowly. I ached with a desire to go home and share my troubles with Ellen. Somehow, I just knew that she would understand. That would be the greatest encouragement of all. But not yet—not until I could clear myself. In the meantime I would try to come up with ideas and study at the library.

I thought of all the people who might help, which lead to an idea. I called George and asked him to call the detective to check on the man who had been sheriff when I disappeared. I knew that he was no longer sheriff, but if he was still living he might help us. He had the reputation of being honest and knowledgeable and he knew almost everyone in the county.

The detective called back, saying that the ex-sheriff was still living and had a good mind. He also said that he knew the ex-sheriff to be trustworthy and suggested the he be hired to help find Dan and Nora if they were still alive.

Did I have money for all of this detective work? I checked with Ellen. She said, "Go ahead and don't worry." I think she would have said this even if we were about to go broke. The ex-sheriff was hired part-time. He already had a lot of knowledge about the case, having investigated it as sheriff. He had always believed that a crime had been committed by Nora and Dan. He mentioned that after leaving the motel where Nora and Dan were I had run my car into a telephone pole. The damage to the car was minor, but I had bumped my forehead against the steering wheel. I had refused first aid and drove off.

At least, my curiosity about this was satisfied. I had by now read so much about amnesia and learned that in almost all cases a blow on the head triggered the loss of memory. This seemed to be true in my case. Maybe I would find out what had brought my memory back.

The ex-sheriff reported that there were hints that Nora might be in contact with her sister and had even written sometimes. One reason for this was that the sister had been very concerned after the disappearance. She often came to the sheriff, blasting him for not finding the murderer, telling him that I was guilty. Later, her tone had changed. She suddenly quit insisting that he look for any of us. She had also quit telling everyone how useless the sheriff was.

The ex-sheriff hinted that he might be able to find out where any letters were postmarked. Our detective surmised that the ex-sheriff might use a method slightly illegal since this would involve the postal department. He also said that this might require some extra money. Remembering the good reputation of the ex-sheriff, I felt sure that he would do nothing actually illegal. Even if he did, we couldn't see how any of us, including the detective, could be involved. George gave the detective the right to spend the extra money, hoping something would come from this.

We had to find Dan and Nora. I didn't believe

that they would ever appear until I was found, knowing that they might be charged with my disappearance. Yet, they might be so money hungry that they would take a chance that nothing could be proved unless my body was found. Another possible charge might be that they had taken money from our partnership.

No way did I dare come out into the open until they were located. It was still a waiting game. No divorce records had yet been found concerning James Heffner's divorce from Nora. They could be anywhere, though. I believed that they existed because if Nora and Dan planned to get the business from me, they would have to be sure that her marriage to me was legal.

The ex-sheriff came up with a little more news. He said that there was a long-time relationship between Dan and Nora, even before I came to Wellsville. Was my whole relationship with her a set-up? She had the authority to write checks and she talked me into taking Dan in as a partner. He had enough money to buy into the company. Maybe they were so sure of their ability that they didn't even bother with a divorce.

This wasn't much, but maybe enough to go back and tell Ellen the story to date. I was so anxious to see my new family. I could hardly believe how Ellen had been so patient in our telephone talks, never insisting that I tell her more, always saying, "Hank, I trust you always. You would never do anything wrong."

I called George and said, "I just have to tell her and let her make a decision. It is only right."

Early the next morning I was on my way. Every mile to South Carolina seemed like ten. I arrived late in the afternoon. Ellen and the children were at home. Such a homecoming! My feelings were mixed. I loved seeing them, but dreaded hearing Ellen's decision. After the dinner the children just stayed on my lap, telling me all of the important things which had happened in my absence. Ellen sometimes found an empty spot on my knee also.

Finally, Ellen put the children to bed. Back in the living room, Ellen took the children's place on my lap. Having this beautiful strange woman so near me almost caused me to lose control, but I managed to gather enough willpower to say, "Ellen, let's go to my office where I can sit across the desk from you and tell you everything. You may never want to sit on my lap again."

She got up, laughing and saying, "I doubt that."

We sat across the desk from each other. I looked her in the eye and said, "The very first thing I have to tell you is that we may not be legally married. I have to know whether you want me to leave now or tell you the whole story."

Ellen never blinked an eye, but said, "If you leave, you will have to fight your way past me first."

I said, "But, Ellen, I may be guilty of bigamy, murder, or embezzlement. I haven't been able to prove anything yet."

Ellen almost exploded, saying, "Hank, haven't I always trusted you? Did I ever question you about your past? I knew from the first that you are a good person. You could never have done anything wrong. Ten years later I am even more sure. Now tell me if you want, but I will trust you even if you don't."

I couldn't believe that I had picked a woman like this, especially after finding a woman like Nora. I told her everything I knew about the trouble I might still be in, offering to get out of her life. Ellen laughed at this, telling how we had met and fallen in love at first sight. Of course, she had taken me on trust. Of course, she had wondered. Her family had wondered and asked. Her only reply to them was that I wouldn't talk about an unpleasant childhood. People had got to know me and just accepted her story.

Then I got enough willpower to suggest that I

sleep in the extra bedroom until we knew whether we were legally married.

With her eyes twinkling, Ellen replied, "Go ahead if you want to, but you are sure going to have company."

The next morning I woke, tapped Ellen on the shoulder and asked, "Was our first honeymoon this good?"

She said, "It sure was. Why?"

I said, "I can't believe that any man deserves two nights like this in one lifetime."

Ellen giggled, saying, "Maybe you haven't seen anything yet."

The next two weeks were spent with Ellen and the children. I got to know my family again. What a great time and a relief from motel rooms. Many things had to be settled about my business. I decided to stay at the house claiming illness. I couldn't believe how much Ellen had learned about the business in such a short time.

Then she told me that my construction foreman had made an offer for my company which she felt was a fair offer. If he could raise the money, this might be an answer, as I had no idea how much money the investigation might take.

The land in Ohio might now be worth several hundred thousand dollars. It could also be years before I would get anything out of it if it was in litigation. I might not appear unless I could prove Dan and Nora were still alive. If I couldn't prove that Nora wasn't my legal wife, she might get half of the land. There was also the possibility that they could claim the land was bought with partnership money. I was intrigued with developing this land. I had a lot of ideas about what would be the best way profit-wise and tax-wise.

I needed to know whether I was responsible for any left-over taxes and penalties. I had George contract the accounting firm which we had employed in the construction business in Wellsville. I knew it might take them a long time to find the information we needed.

Ellen and I decided to sell the business if an agreement could be reached and the buyer could raise the money. Once again accountants were needed. I had been using a firm for years. It didn't take them long to reach a dollar figure. The potential purchaser consulted with bankers who agreed to help finance the purchase. I lowered the price some, then lent him operating cash to provide for one year's expenses.

All this negotiation got real sticky at times. I did not want to admit that I had no memory of what they were talking about. I just had to bluff. I took Ellen everywhere. She knew a lot about the business by now and helped with embarrassing moments by changing the subject or asking a questions about something else. Even though we were proud of how we handled this, I am sure that we left a lot of people puzzled.

One day at the office my secretary asked, "How did your head get? Do you still have that knot on your head?"

I had no idea what in the world she might be talking about. Then I asked, "What do you mean?"

She said, "Don't you remember the vase falling off the bookcase and hitting you on the head the day before you went out of town?"

I sure didn't remember that, but did I remember the headache. I especially remembered the man across the desk and wondering who in the world he might be and where I was. That blow the secretary was telling me about was the other knock on the head that had made me Henry Eller again. This discovery coincided with what I had learned about amnesia. A big part of the mystery about my life was now solved, or seemed to be.

It took a couple of weeks to work out details of the sale of my business, working with my accountant and the bankers. The sale was made, and I found myself with a net worth of nearly $300,000. This included a home without a mortgage and investments. This seemed like a lot of money until I remembered the amount of money I would be paying out to solve my case. The value of the property in Ohio was offset by possible tax debts and the probability that Dan and Nora would try to prove ownership.

Then came another report from the detective. The ex-sheriff had a clue as to where Dan and Nora might be. Someone had sent a letter to a box number in a large city to a person whose name was unfamiliar to him. The ex-sheriff was cagey enough that he wouldn't even tell our detective the name, the city or who sent the letter. He also said the name was only used to receive mail. The detective reasoned that the ex-sheriff was being so secretive because he had gotten the information through questionable means. He passed the information to the detective orally. The detective suggested a meeting. He had a couple of suggestions that he didn't want to discuss by telephone. One suggestion had been made by the ex-sheriff. He had found someone who had known Dan and Nora well. This person had been only fifteen years old when they disappeared and had changed so much that they wouldn't recognize him. He also had some experience in the sheriff's department and might help in some way.

The detective's suggestion, option number two, was that he try to get the post office box number from the ex-sheriff and hire a detective from the city where the box was located to watch for anyone opening the box, then shadowing them to get a picture. George told the detective that he wanted to think about it.

George suggested that I meet with him so I went again to Michigan. There were things that neither the detective or the ex-sheriff knew. For one thing, I was alive.

George called the detective, telling him we had chosen option number two. He said that we needed a picture of the subjects with a witness to verify the date the picture was taken. The detective said he was optimistic and I stayed on "needles and pins."

One of the biggest leads was already off my shoulders, provided by Ellen's reaction to my confession of possible bigamy. She said, "So what? If we are not legally married, you get a divorce and we will try again."

I was really anxious to call my parents, but I had to wait. I was also anxious to appear in Wellsville in the open and really work on the settlement of everything. Once Dan and Nora knew I was alive they would reappear to try to get a part of the land or anything else I might have.

Even though I now had a lot of money, it was sure going out fast and Nora would surely try to get some of it if she could.

George got an optimistic report from my old accountants. According to my old tax returns all company and personal taxes had been paid except for the year of our disappearance. They also thought taxes had been paid on most of the money that had disappeared. This was money held over for operating money.

They might not be able to get the Internal Revenue records without a court order. Naturally the revenue department wouldn't give out records until we proved that not one cent was coming to them.

It was waiting time for me. I went back to South Carolina and the family. I spent the days with Ellen while the children were in school. I got acquainted with Ellen all over again. I was more impressed every day. She was not only beautiful but highly intelligent. How had I picked two women so opposite—the worst, then the best?

We spent the days discussing all of the possibilities of the future on the assumption that Nora and Dan would be found. Then I could appear in the open. We agreed that we would fight to keep Nora and Dan from getting anything even if I got nothing either.

Ellen and I discussed all options and she really came up with some good ideas as we talked. First, Nora might make a claim that she was my wife. This would require her to prove that she was divorced from James Heffner. This wouldn't help me much.

They would, of course, try to prove that the now valuable land had been bought with company money and not my money. Even if this failed, she could claim half as my wife. Dan would probably claim one half as a partner. We thought this claim could be beaten.

Then there was the big question of what had happened to the money which must have disappeared from the company. Where was the $75,000 that I was now convinced I had taken with me? Did I leave a trail or could they prove that I hadn't turned it in to be put in the bank? To prove this, company records would have to be produced. If they were able to produce the books, there would be evidence of money taken after my disappearance. I was sure it might be as much as $300,000. We concluded that tracing this money would be our best course. If they had cashed checks for this amount, there must be records, with signatures on the checks. This would have been legal. On the other hand, this would have been company money. This would more than offset the $75,000 I might have taken.

This was all speculation, as they hadn't even been found yet, but it was interesting and fun for us. It sure kept me busy and gave me little time to be nervous, worrying about whether they would ever be found.

We found it interesting to surmise how Dan and

Nora would make a claim against the valuable property I had bought. Nora might sue me to claim a wife's property rights. It would be hard for them to prove that the money for this property came from the company. Even if they won a claim, they could not sell the land without my cooperation and I did not intend to cooperate.

Then came the good news from George. Our detective reported that the detectives had watched the post office box in Dallas, Texas. By alternating persons watching the box they spotted both a man and woman checking the box several times. They had shadowed them to where they lived, then took pictures with a zoom camera from a car. The ex-sheriff then identified them as Dan and Nora. At last I felt safe enough to come out into the open, but I wanted to see the pictures first.

As anxious as I was to get back to Wellsville, there was one thing I had to do first. That was to see and talk to my parents. I called George and asked him to call them and break the news to lessen the sudden shock. Then I would call.

George said, "As soon as the calls are made, I'm coming to pick you up and I'll go to Florida with you. I wouldn't miss this for anything."

I gave him time to call back. He told me that he had called them, told them about the amnesia and that I was fine. Then he told them that I would call at 11 a.m. This would give them thirty minutes to calm down and to adjust.

It was a long thirty-minute wait for me. At 11 o'clock I called. Dad answered. I said, "Dad, this is Henry."

He answered with his old humor. "Henry, where in the heck have you been? Dinner has been ready for twelve years." Then, "Talk to Mom, before she breaks my arm."

We talked and talked, crying at the same time.

Finally I asked, "Don't you want to talk to your new daughter-in-law?" They talked to Ellen a long time while a lot more tears were shed. She told them that only George and I were coming as the children were in school. Dad said if I didn't bring pictures I would be sent back for them.

George drove in late that night. He had never met Ellen. He made us wake the children so he could meet them. They were sleepy, but he was now Uncle George.

Then I told George that he could sleep in the car while I drove. I couldn't wait any longer to see our parents. We arrived about noon the next day and stayed three days for a great time of remembering. They looked great, of course, but twelve years older and with some worry lines caused by me.

They wanted to know everything about my lost years. They looked at pictures of Ellen and the children. It was impossible to explain why Ellen had married me without knowing my background. I could only say, "Pure blind trust, which led to a miracle for me."

We did explain that when my memory returned, I had to prove that I didn't have deep troubles from the past. Of course, they wouldn't tell old friends about my return until I gave them the word. I wanted to see the picture of Dan and Nora first, even though I felt certain that the ex-sheriff had to recognize them. Mom kept telling me to call the minute I could. Dad advised me to invest in telephone stock as Mom would be spending a lot of money making calls back to old friends in Pennsylvania.

Our family had had a great warm relationship—hunting, fishing camping. Our parents had followed us in sports, one or both of them going to every game we ever played if possible. Yet, nothing in the past ever equaled our three-day reunion. We didn't discuss details of my troubles. I just said, "Wait until I see one more picture. I am anxious to tell you everything. You will find it interesting." They were patient, as always.

I sure hated to leave, but I was so anxious to get back to Dayton to see the pictures. George had taken a few days' vacation and I would need him.

After our goodbyes, mixed with more tears, we headed back north, stopping to see Ellen and the children. When we reached Dayton, George told our detective to pick up the pictures. He told George that other people had now seen the pictures identifying Dan and Nora, but I still had to see them for myself. As I expected, there was no doubt. I could make myself known. We now had the names they were using and their addresses.

I met the detective for the first time. I dismissed him, telling him that this might be a long drawn-out affair. I mentioned that we might have to prove that Dan and Nora had arrived in Texas with money. I also told him exactly where this now valuable land was located. I sure didn't tell him it had only existed in my mind when he was first told about it. I felt that he might resent George's not leveling with him.

He did say that he had heard rumors about this and had a few clues to follow if needed. I hoped that my old accountants might be able to help. In any case, I no longer needed this detective. Neither did I need the detectives in Texas nor the ex-sheriff any longer. When I paid all the costs it was not a huge amount. I still had most of my money to live on and money for accountants and court battles.

George went back to work. It was up to me now. I felt ready for battle. I went to Wellsville and got a motel room. There I got a big lift by suddenly realizing that I could now call Ellen as often as I wanted. I could call my parents. I could call George or anyone else without being tricky in telephone booths. Before I even unpacked, I called Ellen. When she said, "Hello," I said, "Is this Mrs. Henry Eller?" This left her speechless for a moment. She still thought she was Mrs. Henry Thompson. Taking advantage of her silence, I boasted, "This is

Henry Eller. I am staying at Knights Inn in Wellsville, Ohio. My telephone number is available when you want to call me."

Then we both laughed, happy that I could now call her or anyone when I wanted to call. I now felt liberated. I could go where I wanted, talk to anyone, renew old acquaintances from my days in construction. One of the first persons I went to see was the ex-sheriff. He was happy that his unsolved case was concluded, even though it was no longer his responsibility. I told him about the valuable property and asked him to spread the word to bring Dan and Nora into the open. He agreed that the smell of money would surely do this. Even if court costs would be expensive, I wanted the case settled.

I visited the new owners of my old construction company. Some of my old employees were still with them. We had a nice little reunion. The new owners didn't know much about the old records except that the courts had cleared the titles so that they could buy the company.

I next called on my old accountants. They had only turned in quarterly and end-of-the-year reports and didn't keep our books. They only saw them at these times. Then to my old real estate estate agency and the valuable property. Was he ever upset! Why had I never contacted him? I told him to be patient for awhile. I wasn't even sure I would sell the land as long as I believed Dan and Nora might profit from it.

I was really intrigued with the possibilities. It would have been so good to develop the land my own way, one part at a time, leasing it, then another part. That way one area could finance the next.

It meant more than money. This was my life's work—the only thing in my life from boyhood that I loved to do and now I had to wait, at least until Dan and Nora made their appearance and entered claims on the property.

Through all of these visits I never mentioned

amnesia. I had no particular reason for this except that everyone would have wanted to spend most of our time talking about this. There was also the possibility that this could be part of a court case later.

Then back to Newburg, South Carolina and a family that was still new to me. We were going to live it up. I was looking forward to visiting my parents in Florida. I wanted to take Ellen and the children to meet them. I looked forward to telling my mom and dad the whole story. Ellen could tell them the story of the "lost years." Then they could tell their story of how they and brother George searched for me.

There might be long months of claims and lawsuits by Dan and Nora and I would respond. I was no longer concerned about bigamy. If Nora could prove that we were still married, Ellen and I could just get married again after a divorce.

In the meantime we would just live it up, meeting old friends and new people. The children were excited about having new grandparents and cousins.

When things finally got a little boring, I was sure that Dan and Nora would provide excitement. For the time being it was, "Let's think about that later."